I

HEAR

YOUR

VOICE

Also by Young-ha Kim

I HAVE THE RIGHT TO DESTROY MYSELF

YOUR REPUBLIC IS CALLING YOU

BLACK FLOWER

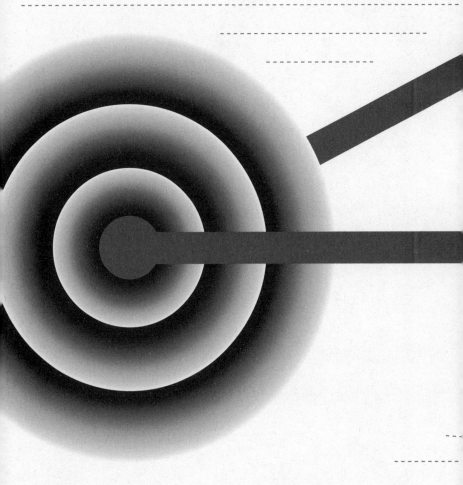

MARINER

I HEAR

YOUNG-HA KIM

Translated by KRYS LEE

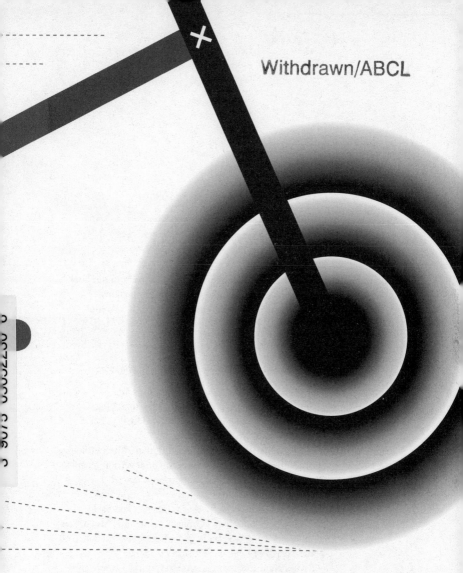

YOUR VOICE

MARINER BOOKS · HOUGHTON MIFFLIN HARCOURT

BOSTON   NEW YORK

First Mariner Books edition 2017

WWW.HMHCO.COM

First published by Munhakdongne Publishing Group, 2012

Library of Congress Cataloging-in-Publication Data
Names: Kim, Young-ha, date, author. | Lee, Krys, translator.
Title: I hear your voice / Young-ha Kim ; translated by Krys Lee.
Other titles: Nŏ ŭi moksori ka tŭllyŏ.
English Description: First Mariner Books edition. | Boston : Mariner Books,
2017. | Translated from Korean. | Description based on print version record and
CIP data provided by publisher; resource not viewed.
Identifiers: LCCN 2017018690 (print) | LCCN 2016055934 (ebook) |
ISBN 9780544324480 (ebook) | ISBN 9780544324473 (paperback)
Subjects: LCSH: Teenage boys — Fiction. | Orphans — Fiction. | Motorcycle
gangs — Fiction. | Friendship — Fiction. | Seoul (Korea) — Fiction. |
BISAC: FICTION / Literary. | FICTION / General.
Classification: LCC PL992.415.Y5863 (print) |
LCC PL992.415.Y5863 N613 2017 (ebook) | DDC 895.7/34 — dc23
LC record available at https://lccn.loc.gov/2017018690

Book design by Mark R. Robinson

PRINTED IN THE UNITED STATES OF AMERICA
DOC 10 9 8 7 6 5 4 3 2 1

PART
ONE

A ROPE DESCENDS FROM THE SKY, SO THE BEGIN-
ning itself is strange. But since it's only the beginning, the audience withholds judgment. A solemn-faced magician tells his
assistant to go up the rope, and at his command, the fearful,
hesitant young man begins climbing. He climbs and climbs.
He continues upward, his small frame becoming even smaller,
until he disappears from view.

The magician shouts into the air, "Now it's time to come
back down!"

There is no response. The magician says, louder, "I told you
to come down. Can you hear me?"

When he still gets no response, the audience grows even
more curious. Where on earth does this rope lead? And what
happened to the kid who went up moments ago? Has he arrived at another world, reached the mysterious place that we
call heaven?

The magician angrily grabs the rope and begins pulling himself up until soon enough, he also disappears from view. Those
gazing up begin to get neck pains and start to feel the weight of
the distant sky. Then, from that high-up place, the young assistant's arms, legs, head, and torso fall — one at a time, without
warning. Straight after, a dull thud, and blood splatters on the
marble floor, as if someone just knocked over a wineglass on a
white tablecloth. It is red and violent and chaotic. The audi-

ence recoils, shocked. Then the magician returns down the rope with his hands coated in blood, his face frozen with anger. He retrieves his assistant's scattered body parts and puts them into a bucket. After shoving it behind him, he gazes contemptuously at the terrified audience, as if to say: What else do you want?

Just then a sound comes from behind the magician. The straw mat covering the bucket lifts, and — as if emerging from a long nap — the boy rubs his eyes as he arises. The magician is more nonchalant than shocked, as if crossing the boundary between life and death is no big deal. The boy vanishes; the vanished boy dies; the dead boy comes back to life. For the sake of audience members still skeptical of his resurrection, the limber boy does some handsprings until everyone feels reassured that he is definitely alive. Blood is coursing through his arms and legs, and his muscles and joints are functioning properly. Only then does the audience begin clapping wildly.

The first person to document this act of magic was a man named Ibn Battutah. The Marco Polo of the Islamic world, he witnessed this amazing feat in Hangzhou at the end of the Yuan dynasty and wrote about it in his massive travelogue. Although the secrets to countless tricks are now known, the rope act is still a mystery.

A similar tale also exists in China. It is said that a young Chinese emperor witnessed and was deceived by the same act. He was delighted to be so thoroughly tricked and, captivated by the astonishing act of magic, he wanted to see more. So when he turned his attention to the eunuch fanning him, his guards dragged the trembling eunuch forward.

The emperor reassured him, "There's no need to worry. The magician will soon bring you back to life."

An aged attendant spoke up and tried to dissuade the emperor, saying what had happened was nothing more than a trick of the eye. But the emperor ignored him, and said, "We will only know for certain if we try."

Overwhelmed with curiosity, he ordered a massive soldier to approach the eunuch and brandish his sword. A rainbow flashed in the fountain of blood. The magician turned away from the bloody scene and quickly climbed up the rope. After he hid behind the clouds, the rope fell twitching to the ground. It resembled a legendary serpent that had tried to become a dragon and ascend to heaven, but failed.

When I first heard this old tale, I only wondered where the magician had gone. But now I think about the assistant and what happened to him after the magician vanished, leaving him there alone, soaked in the eunuch's blood.

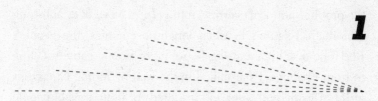

A FRESH-FACED TEENAGER STRAINED TO PUSH THE
shopping cart. In some ways it looked as if the cart were dragging her. She had zipped shut the backpack in the cart and had
her earphones on. She would have resembled one of the homeless people living in the bus terminal if it weren't for her age; she
lacked the hard-boiled look of someone who had lived a long,
difficult life. Though her arms were thin, her upper body was on
the plump side, and her carelessly slipped-on sneakers dragged
across the ground.

The Express Bus Terminal was a nightmare dreamed up by
the massive city of Seoul: a place of hoarse-throated religious fanatics and male prostitutes selling themselves for small change,
beggars missing both their legs singing hymns, con men target-
ing the simple-minded from the provinces, prostitutes without
a regular beat, teenage runaways, a cult leader who believed
in the coming of aliens, hucksters, and purse snatchers; all of
them loathing one another. Behind the fake monk who begged
while tapping at a wooden gong, a man traded in his kidney,
and another man — whose early ejaculation problems made
him unable to satisfy his hot-blooded wife — paid an unlicensed
Asian medicine doctor for a white, powdery treatment with du-
bious powers. Doomsday believers, who trusted that on Judgment Day only the faithful would be saved, positioned themselves throughout the terminal. According to their prophet,

October 28, 1992, would be Judgment Day. Back then, many of the prophets stank of overripe, rotting fruit. News of establishing diplomatic relations between longtime enemies, the People's Republic of China and the Republic of Korea, came trickling in from the large TV installed in the waiting room. Thousands of buses came and went and hundreds of thousands of people swerved past one another.

Almost no one paid attention to the girl. A sole elderly drunk man leered at her, but as soon as she pushed her cart into the bathroom, he lost interest.

She went to a handicap stall and pushed the cart inside. After locking the door and grabbing her backpack, she sat on the toilet seat and withdrew a disposable adult diaper from the pack. She struggled out of her sweatsuit and put it in the cart. As soon as she released the mercilessly tightened maternity belt, her swollen belly sagged out. She pulled off the wet diaper she'd worn beneath her underwear and tossed it into the trashcan. A foul stench overwhelmed the stall. She wiped her sweaty forehead and checked her watch. She took some short, deep breaths and an occasional deliberate heave, but her breathing soon turned irregular. It was as if a skilled torturer occasionally left her alone then returned on impulse.

Used diapers piled up in the trashcan as hot fluid continued seeping from her. The floor became wet. The girl went limp as she watched the amniotic fluid soak her knees and ankles, then finally swirl down a drain clogged with hair. She screamed as pain swept over her again.

Before her echoing screams faded, someone opened the bathroom door and entered. The girl held her breath and stopped up her mouth with her fist. The person went into another stall and immediately flushed the toilet. A lighter was flicked, then smoke drifted over into the girl's stall. Finally the person flushed the toilet again, slammed the stall door shut, and hurried out.

The pauses between contractions became shorter. The girl was seized by fear that the pain would last forever, and was surrendering to the savage monster ripping into her lower belly with thousands of sharp toenails, when a hot energy surged from the crown of her head to her feet. The pain disappeared as if it had never existed. As if it had swirled down some unstopped hole.

She just managed to stay propped up by resting on the toilet, gazing with glassy eyes down at the strange living being dangling from her body. The creature covered in blood and amniotic fluid kept quivering its mouth, but it wasn't crying. The folds around its eyes twitched. The girl needed to finish before it got noisy. She had barely managed to bend and pick up the clammy thing when she wavered. She steeled herself and removed scissors from the backpack, disinfected them with a disposable lighter, and cut the umbilical cord. She threw the lighter into the trashcan but missed, so it rolled across the floor. When she lifted the baby, he started crying.

Like sewage during the rainy season surging upward and pushing past manhole covers, the cry eddied around the stall, filled the bathroom, spilled into the raucous terminal, and swept over the crowds. The girl clamped her hand over the baby's mouth but it was useless. The people exposed to the melancholy scream shuddered. In a space where the only code of conduct toward strangers was indifference, a strange, sudden shame seized them. In the newborn baby's cry was a spell that hit each individual's guilty conscience, and it sent a strong warning: save him from eminent tragedy, or else. Everyone stampeded like a startled herd of cows in the direction of the cry.

Before the girl's delicate, bloodstained hand could smother the baby's last breath, before she could put to sleep that fierce will to live, they swarmed in. A man kicked the door open, and the flimsy hinge flew into the air. If it weren't for the fierce cries, like an awl piercing their ears, the crowd would have assumed they were witnessing a brutal murder scene, since the floor was soaked with the girl's bloody secretions and amniotic fluid. The crowd, agitated by the smell of blood, screamed like monkeys. The flurry of their arms and legs resembled the sudden incarnation of a Hindu god.

A police car and an ambulance arrived quickly. The paramedic tranquilized the girl lying on the stretcher, who soon passed out. Her mind was transported to the two-story house of her childhood, herself asleep in a crib. A dark thundercloud hovered over. Was it about to rain, she wondered, as she continued gazing up. When the ambulance arrived at the emergency room, nurses easily lifted her and moved her to a bed. The girl suddenly looked around. Where is the bloody creature I was just holding? She didn't remember seeing it in the ambulance. What was it called, that squishy, clammy body that cried so loudly? A jumble of words stirred and moved restlessly in her foggy brain. Then a word swam to the surface.

"The baby, where is the baby?" she screamed, rising from the bed until a young intern pushed her back down.

2

NEXT TO THE EXPRESS BUS TERMINAL THERE'S AN enormous plant and flower market that meets the entire city's demand for flowers. It's a place where plants are constantly on the move. Flowers collected here from greenhouses across the country are sent out to the city's flower shops, wedding halls, graduation ceremonies, and funerals. People are born, study, mate, become ill, and die, and flowers are present for all those critical moments. Withered flowers are uniformly despised. They aren't welcome beside a corpse, a newlywed couple, or a recent graduate. Fresh cut flowers — the sexual organs of plants removed from their roots — have to be rushed to their intended destination.

Mama Pig had raised Jae. I'm not sure when Mama Pig became her name, but it stuck even though she had never been married or had a baby, and didn't look at all like a pig. She was slender for her age and had a small appetite. She ran a little shop in one corner of the flower market that sold coffee and other beverages, toast and hard-boiled eggs, snacks and ramen. Her main customers were flower merchants and delivery people, who swallowed a whole fried egg on toast, then loaded large floral wreaths onto a motorbike and raced off. Seen from behind, these enormous wreaths seemed to propel themselves on wheels.

While Jae was thrust out into the world in the bus terminal bathroom, Mama Pig was returning from the bank. She was swept along with the crowd galloping like a herd of wildebeests on the Serengeti Plain. Moments later, she ended up in the chaos of the bathroom. Someone handed her the slippery baby who had just tumbled out from his mother. The baby, having escaped his fate of infanticide, stopped wailing as soon as he landed in her arms. He gazed up at her. Later she recalled how it was if she were a barber holding a razor blade to him. She took the baby to her shop, and after she washed him in warm water and wrapped him in a clean cloth, she held him to herself. Though a distant uproar continued in the bathroom, no one seemed interested in the baby. She closed up shop early that day.

As soon as they arrived home, Mama Pig's three-year-old poodle smelled something new and began yapping as it bounded up and down. She took off her wet blouse and held her breasts with both hands.

"How's this possible?" she said. "Milk, from a virgin's breast!"

While bathing the baby, Mama Pig discovered something strange on his back. She traced the bones bulging out around his shoulder-blade area on both sides, but the baby didn't seem to feel pain and just beamed.

THREE YEARS AFTER BRINGING JAE HOME, MAMA

Pig closed down her little shop and began working for a hostess club's kitchen in Gangnam. Around that time they moved into my family's multi-unit. We had just built an extension to our old two-story house and converted it into six separate apartments. Two families each moved into the second and third floors, and one family moved into the semi-basement. We lived on the first floor. My mother grumbled that we'd gone even deeper into debt because of the high construction costs. A working-class family from Pakistan lived in the semi-basement, a young bachelor and an asthmatic old man lived on the third floor, and Jae's family as well as a Chinese-food delivery man rented the apartments on the second floor.

My first memory of Jae as a kid is him teetering on a dining chair with his arms outstretched when, with an ear-splitting cry, he fell in my direction. I don't remember a grownup running to help him or take him to a hospital; I just remember him falling and a dull pain nailing me to the floor. I assumed that Jae recalled what happened and later often asked him about it, but each time he shook his head. It felt somehow unfair that I remembered the accident more vividly than Jae, when it had happened to him. Maybe he had passed out, or it had happened when he was so young that he had just forgotten. But whenever I think about him, this scene appears before me like a movie theater preview. This memory — maybe even a fake memory I made up much later — came back along with a jumble of sensations. When Jae standing at that high place loses his balance and totters, my heart starts pounding and my head goes numb. From somewhere a whirring sound begins, like a fan that's lost one of its wings turning at high speed, and my hands go slick with sweat. My breath shortens, and a faint smell of something like gasoline permeates. I, of all people, can't deny this memory. It's stayed with me through all these sensations. What I mean is, I'm sure they aren't images from a movie that have accidentally sneaked in.

The crescent-shaped scar on Jae's forehead was likely from that fall. Throughout his life, whenever he was thinking, he rubbed at the scar with his index finger, as if scrubbing the fuzz from an eraser. He falls toward me over and over again. His backlit silhouette, both arms stretched out to me to pin me down inside fear and pain.

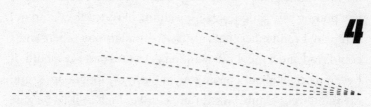

4

WHEN WE WERE AROUND FOUR YEARS OLD, MY UN-
cle took Jae and me out to the riverside. We had a remote-controlled miniature helicopter with us. At first we had fun watching it whir around. Jae and I probably clapped and laughed, maybe we even ran after it with our hands extended. But suddenly my uncle steered it in my direction. That was the first time I experienced — no, that was the first time I remember — feeling panicked. Maybe I thought the enormous whirring object was attacking me. Even now when I close my eyes, I can see its dragonfly-like compound eyes filled with evil, circling toward me. When I shuddered and shrank away, my uncle quickly sent the helicopter in another direction. Dogs out on their walks barked noisily and followed the helicopter; their owners watched, amused. I was the only one terrified.

Jae was different from me. His eyes burned holes through the helicopter as if determined to move it telepathically. I don't think he blinked. Like a catatonic patient at some mental hospital who stands in the same place all day, he tensed his arms and legs as he focused on the floating helicopter. His odd stillness stopped my crying. I started to wonder if he was actually communicating with the helicopter.

I'm not sure whether I stopped talking before or after that day. But I definitely have no memories of saying anything out loud for a long time after that. The taste of terror is still vivid for me, like a giant pair of tongs squeezing my brain (it tastes like putting your tongue against a chunk of rusted iron). I'm not sure why I remember that as a taste. I understood others and I could read and write. I just couldn't get words past my mouth. If I even thought about opening my mouth, my tongue froze and my mind went blank. Words were elusive. I felt as if I'd be able to speak if I tried hard, or if I tried a little more, but at that point my heart would palpitate and my fists would slicken with sweat, and finally I'd realize there was no way I'd be able to speak and I would fall silent. It was the same feeling you get when a nightmare paralyzes you. My mother said I spoke just fine until I was three, but sometime after that I spoke less and less until eventually I was always silent, even with her. But that's only her version. I remember being a child who had never said a word.

The helicopter brings back another story connected to my uncle. About that time he decided to join the police force and moved to Seoul to study. He had just completed national service so at most he was about twenty-two or twenty-three. My uncle was the reticent type and came off as crude. I'd never really been keen on him, and likewise he'd never cared much for me. He went to classes during the day and studied in private reading rooms at night, but he ate breakfast and dinner at our house. My father was a plainclothes detective who often didn't come home for days. Sometimes he returned stinking, probably from the fine layer of tear gas that came from shutting down a protest. I associate my father with this smell. The vague memory of him staggering into the house late at night, and the acrid smell and the violent energy that came with him — that alone was enough to put me on edge.

My uncle kept me company when my father wasn't home,

but I don't remember it being much fun. He stayed in the house-keeping room connected to the kitchen; he despised it when I burst in, and he threw a fit each time. You could reach it only through a small door connected to the kitchen, and when the door was shut, this isolated room looked like another storage room. Because of its unusual location, I was startled each time he emerged. To a young kid like me, it looked like a secret door to another world. When my uncle was in classes I would sneak into the room, where a smell of damp laundry and sour, rotting fruit clung to the walls. For some reason he had glued glow-in-the-dark stars to the ceiling, so if you turned off the lights the Big Dipper radiated. It was amazing to me, so I'd go into the room and switch the lights on and off.

My uncle passed the exam and became a police officer. Before the results were officially announced, my father called home, thrilled that his little brother would also join the police force. I still remember the sizzle of splattering oil, the rank, burning fat, and the mushiness of overcooked roasted pork belly. Jae had come downstairs for a free meal, Mom was bustling in the kitchen, and my father had returned from work excited, making a fuss. I was five years old, hiding behind the sofa and staring up at my uncle. I remember being confused by the stark contrast between his cheerful expression around my father and his usual cold, cynical look. It was probably the first time I'd recognized a person with a secret.

Unlike your typical cop, my father couldn't hold his liquor, and early on he fell asleep drunk. Jae and I huddled in front of the TV and watched cartoons. My uncle was bent over the grill, eating pieces of cold meat until he suddenly rose and said, "I better go now."

My mother saw him out. His huge duffle bag, stuffed with his belongings, hung at a stiff angle as if it were furious about something. I raised myself up from behind the sofa and gazed at the front door. It was then that my uncle's hand struck her. The arm hidden by his body seemed to stretch out, slowly draw a semicircle in the air, and target her cheek. *Smaack*, I still hear it now. A surreal, sharp, unpleasant sound.

Oh, it's Inspector Gadget! I thought. Up to that point, I'd still believed that the two adults were playing around. But he didn't stop, and hit my mother's cheek again. I couldn't tell what it might mean for her to take two slaps in silence, but it felt ominous, and I had a hunch it was dangerous. There was no sign of my father. Before I knew it, I'd started to stand up, but Jae yanked me back down by the arm. He touched his index finger to his lips and signaled me to be quiet. His eerie grown-up watchfulness that day made me uncomfortable.

We turned back to the TV, but our bodies were completely tuned in to what was happening out front. Soon my uncle slammed the front door behind him. My mother cleared the table and began washing dishes. Sometimes the clinking of dishes would suddenly stop and leave a troubling silence. But I couldn't bear to sneak glances at my mom's back, so Jae and I fixed our eyes on the TV and blankly watched the screen.

My uncle visited several times after that, and he and my mother got along fine — as if nothing had happened. Each time, I wondered whether what I'd seen had actually happened. I continued not to speak. No one seemed to consider these symptoms serious; they just thought of me as a quiet kid. That is, until the kindergarten teacher called my mother and told her that I had a problem. My mother must have known that something wasn't right but maybe wasn't ready to face it, reassuring herself every day: he'll be fine tomorrow, it's probably nothing.

Not long after that, the battles between my dad and mom began. They were violent fights. They hurled nasty words at each other and threw dishes that would break against the wall. I was afraid that they would completely forget I existed. Years later I saw a videotaped scene from my parents' wedding, with a young man and woman, harboring great hopes for the future, beaming and greeting their guests. I realized that in a world where I didn't exist, they had been happy. Did I have to disappear for them to return to that original state? Maybe they were happy not *despite* my absence, but *because* of my absence. Weighed down by those heavy thoughts, I quickly turned off the video.

I wasn't able to attend kindergarten because I didn't speak, so I spent the days stuck at home rereading picture books or playing alone, making up stories about my toys. My mother left a measured distance between us, like a boxer who jabs at his opponent to hold him at bay. I have almost no memories of her hugging me or ruffling my hair in affection. She treated me as if I were a neighbor's pet she was dog-sitting. I was a guest who had arrived in the wrong place at the wrong time, and I became sure I was unwanted. Words slowly started to rise inside me but still I didn't speak. No, I *couldn't* speak. Jae was the only person who stuck by me.

I had functional aphonia, an anxiety-related illness — but no one knew to call it this. Later, when I learned that my suffering had a name, that alone was a relief, since it meant I wasn't the only one, that others had the same condition.

But Jae didn't treat me as if I were weird. We would silently spend half the day together on the jungle gym or roam the neighborhood for a while, then go home and watch TV. It was as if he had said, You don't have to speak if you don't want to.

Mama Pig didn't leave for work until late in the afternoon and returned home near midnight. Sometimes Jae and I tagged along with her to the hostess club. This was before the financial crisis and the currency meltdown, so the economy was still strong and Mama Pig had hardly any days off. If a regular asked for a snack that wasn't on the menu, she had to make it for him, from Beolgyo cockles to marinated and grilled dried pollock. She also had to make hangover stew for a private room packed with raging drunk customers.

Mama Pig would often say, "Rich people don't want what everyone else wants. They're choosy and quick-tempered. That's what the rich are like."

She had grown up by the sea, so she had a way of cooking that made her popular with customers. A regular who owned several buildings in the heart of the Gangnam district said that he didn't come for the alcohol, but for the food.

"That's crazy," said Mama Pig. "Our customers spend enough to buy a car in one visit alone, and he says he comes to eat."

She clicked her tongue in disapproval, but she didn't seem to feel too bad about it, since afterward she often repeated to other customers what he'd said.

When I breathe in deeply, I can smell the hostess club even now. Just down the stairs to the club's basement location, the smells formed a wall that separated it from the rest of the world. On top of a thick layer of bleach, there was a faint scent of freesia, jasmine, and lavender air freshener, and over that, a strong animal scent swirled around like cream in coffee. This strange world replete with powerfully artificial smells resembled the entrance into a secret temple. Low-lit halogen lamps illuminated the black-and-sienna minimalist interior; I used to stare in wonder at their timid light as it fell on the carpet like a first snow. You could peek at the entrance from a narrow hallway connecting the kitchen and the storage area.

Every day when it opened for business, men in bowties lined up with their eyes to the ground. There wasn't a woman in sight; the women stayed shrouded in darkness, drunk on their own beauty; then, as if greeting distinguished guests, they suddenly rushed out with bright smiles. After they led their first customers to private rooms, the madam gave alcohol to the bowtied men who were still waiting and sent them to the bar. All night long the madam sent the girls from one room to the next. When I think back on the hostess club, I imagine a medieval convent I'd once seen in a movie. Girls in black would covertly move between the locked doors of secret rooms, and men with money and power would visit them. Even with the eruptions of loud voices and blasts of music, the hostess club had a surprising ascetic energy. So despite the presence of beautiful women, everything felt taboo except drinking. With its spare interior and marble floors, the hostess club wasn't a cheap red-light-district space and actually had the air of a well-decorated executive's office. The women, done up like secretaries, attended to men who demonstrated remarkable restraint.

Once, when the madam discovered Jae and me running in

the hallway, she grabbed us by the ear and warned, "If the customers see you, I'll kick you all out."

When Mama Pig heard about this, she added another warning: "Listen to madam auntie. The customers are paying a fortune to get away from kids like you. If they wanted to be around kids, they'd stay home. Why would they come here?"

Jae and I roamed everywhere except the reception area and the private rooms. We would get free late-night snacks in the kitchen, play hide-and-seek in the liquor storage, then fall asleep in the waiters' lodgings. In the rank disorder of their beds, we saw the bare face of the poor. Within the hostess club's temple of beauty, the stench of poverty crept out from the armpits of the young men. One of the waiters, who went by the name of Popeye, called Jae and me mice because he said we were always scrambling in and out. His right forearm was crowded with blue tattoos. Sometimes he rolled up his sleeve and showed them off to us, flexing his muscles so the letters on his arm wiggled like bugs.

Sometimes the women embraced us. When their warm breath brushed across my neck, I went hard. A woman's hands that entertained men every day had special energy. Even now, I like being held so tightly I can barely breathe, though I know that no one can help me relive the crude excitement I'd felt as a six-year-old kid. When you repeatedly realize that all your new experiences utterly pale against the brilliance of the past, life becomes underwhelming. I learned that all too quickly.

For a while I believed that all young women were slender because of my time in the club, despite the exceptions I witnessed there. One chubby, cranky woman would pinch our cheeks or slap our butts whenever she saw us. We tried to avoid the witch, but she tracked us down like a bloodhound. She reeked of alcohol as she pretended to eat us alive and tugged at our ears. Once Jae made a run in her pantyhose with his fingernail, and then she really did rage like a witch. Women in that line of work believed getting a run in your pantyhose or breaking a fingernail was unlucky.

Once, Popeye and the witch entered the storage room as we were reading a comic book in a cozy hideout we'd made by moving around crates of alcohol. They didn't know we were there, and began caressing each other. The cases of alcohol stacked up on the pallet rattled and clanked like a train. At first the lovers folded close together and swayed like tall seagrass, but their movements intensified. When the witch began screaming, Popeye covered her mouth. Slowly their movements subsided. Their bodies, dangerously entwined, straightened. Like a dog shaking rain off his coat, they noisily tidied up and, one at a time, exited. It was like theater. One actor appeared after the other, passionately delivered his or her lines, then walked off the stage. I still see that somehow tragic-looking piece of flesh that hung from Popeye's body dangling in front of me. I didn't think of it as just a body part. Popeye gazed down at it and, as if to say "You've worked hard," tapped at it with his right hand, then lifted up his pants in one swoop. When the dangling flesh disappeared into his body like a snake's tongue, I held my breath.

The accident that got us exiled from paradise also happened in that storage room. One day I was in the hideout, lost in a comic book until I saw that Jae had somehow climbed to the top of the stacked crates of Scotch. I gestured for him to come down, but he ignored me. Instead, as if seeking someone higher up, he extended his right hand and slowly stood up. He wavered, readying to jump to a tower of beer crates one leap away. As I zigzagged up the crates to help him down, he lost his balance and began tottering. Squatting with both arms apart, he looked like a dancer coerced by authorities into performing. The tower tilted, so Jae stooped and clutched at the crates with both hands, but the tower only leaned farther. Bottles of seventeen-year-old Scotch thundered as they rolled everywhere. Only when the tower tumbled did Jae look to me for help. He flew in the opposite direction of the whiskey crates. Meaning, he fell on me. The floor was soaked, and the cloying smell of expensive whiskey stung our noses and made us dizzy. The cold liquid seeping into my shirt felt like blood. Popeye rushed in and picked up Jae — who was knocked out and lying on top of me — and carried him out. One virtue of people in the bar trade: no matter how terrible the accident, they stay cool-headed. Popeye silently discarded the glass shards and wiped up the whiskey with a rag. But from his quick glance my way, I sensed he wasn't unhappy about the disaster awaiting us. When the madam arrived, I was dragged to the bathroom, stripped of my whiskey-drenched clothes, and forced to shower. She threw a promo T-shirt with a Chivas Regal logo at me and said, "Game's over. Don't show up here anymore. Got it?"

Mama Pig had never traveled abroad. She was the kind who wouldn't have known whether Guam was in the Pacific Ocean or the Atlantic. If Korean Air flight 801 hadn't hit heavy rains on August 6, 1997, and rashly attempted to land at Guam's international airport in Agana, that island never would have played a part in her life. During a storm the landing equipment had malfunctioned; that, on top of poor judgment by the pilots. Near the airport, the Boeing 747 collided with Nimitz Hill; included among its 254 passengers were the man who owned the hostess club and the witch. Mama Pig watched the TV news flashes like she'd gone mad, muttering that she couldn't understand why out of all the club's beautiful women, the owner had gone on vacation with the witch.

The new owner of the hostess club had extensive renovations done and replaced the madam. Of course the new madam brought her own people with her, and the kitchen was no exception. So Mama Pig lost her job.

Even well into the future, whenever Jae and I ran out of things to talk about, we ended up describing the hostess bar to each other as if it were an elusive utopia. It housed an unlimited supply of food. When a slip of paper passed through a small hole, it was transformed into a bounty of alcohol and snacks, including all sorts of fruit and dried seafood, American beef jerky and dried nuts, which dexterous waiters carried into the rooms. Then finally, the waiters demonstrated a nearly acrobatic, effortless ability to silently uncap dozens of beer bottles with one hand.

One waiter said, "If you make any noise at all, some customers will tell you not to open the bottles. Before they notice, you have to quietly open them all."

Bewitching women with long fingernails, a feast of snacks, unfinished and discarded bottles of Scotch and cognac, bourbon and beer piled as high as a mountain. Hefty doormen who lifted us up high in the air whenever they saw us. The hostess club must have had a gang backing it as well as public officials hunting for violations and demanding bribes; on top of that some messy, horrifying events probably happened behind the scenes, but we knew nothing about any of this.

Soon after the club changed hands, Jae started at a regular elementary school and I went off to a school for kids with special needs. Because we lived in the same house, we still hung out in the afternoons. We shared a special bond that baffled other kids. Jae instantly understood the words slowed up inside me that wouldn't rush past my lips, that stayed petrified like stalactites. So he began speaking for me. At first I was amazed — it was similar to moving objects through telekinesis — but later I took it for granted. Jae didn't get every single one of my thoughts in one try, but he figured them out within a few attempts. Sometimes when Jae made off-the-wall guesses, I would either give up or start wanting whatever Jae wanted. Yes — I would lie to myself. Jae got a high from reading my desires, and I didn't want to destroy that illusion. He wasn't the receiver of my desires; he was their interpreter.

5

ONE SUNDAY WE WERE WATCHING A FOREIGN FILM

on TV about a man who plotted to destroy a rival magician. During a magic trick in which the rival's assistant was to loosen her bindings and emerge safely from a tank full of water, the man made sure the tank was locked. When the woman, whom the rival loved, didn't emerge on time, he pushed aside the drapes. He frantically bashed at the tank as his lover struggled for her life, but it was useless. Mere centimeters separated the two, but one was surrounded by water and the other by air. Her words, trapped in the tank, couldn't escape. The two lovers couldn't even touch hands. Only their gaze connected the wide-eyed woman, drifting like a jellyfish, and the man frozen in despair. That scene absorbed me until I was unable to follow the rest of the story. It felt as if tiny poisonous bubbles were frothing in all my body's cells and riding through the blood vessels up to my head. My whole world turned purple. I reached for the remote control and turned off the TV. As soon as the sound stopped, my mother, who had been trimming bean sprouts, looked up.

"Mommy," I said.

"What?"

She didn't seem to realize what had just happened.

"Mommy."

"What is it, for heaven's sake?"

"I don't want to watch anymore."

Only then did my mother scramble up from her seat.

"You, you spoke? Can you do it again, please?"

I kept quiet and held back my tears, but after my mother grabbed me and began shaking me by the shoulders, I had to say, "Stop shaking me. I'm fine."

She said I would be transferred right away from the special needs school to a regular school. I immediately resented having spoken. It was as if I'd been tricked into losing something important to me. What was so great about being able to speak? I already had friends at the special needs school. They were comfortable with my silence, and I had rapidly become good at sign language. When I first saw kids using sign language, I was mesmerized by their quick, elaborate hand movements that seemed to create invisible birds and release them into the air.

The next day my mother rushed me to school. At the time I was obsessed with Aesop's fables and would turn the day's events into a kind of fable. In my story that day my mother was a greedy owner and I was an old donkey. Everyone, listen to this old tale. A fat, greedy owner dragged her old donkey to the market. Look here, he said, I have a talking donkey. At the market they didn't believe him, saying, Nah, how can a donkey talk? I've never heard anything so absurd in my life! No, this donkey is different. I mean, yesterday he suddenly began speaking like a human! The merchants crowded in. That's amazing. They said, Make it speak. The owner poked the donkey's side. Startled, the donkey brayed. The merchants cocked their heads. Isn't that just a typical donkey cry? The greedy owner grabbed the donkey and began reasoning with it. I'm begging you, speak like a human, if only not to disgrace me. Seeing its owner's tears, the donkey weakened and finally said a few words. The merchants were startled and the owner, exultant, said, Now, how much are you willing to pay? I'll have to charge a high sum for a talking donkey. But the merchants shook their heads. Nah, what use is a talking donkey? If you make it work, it'll complain. It'll make fun of its owner behind his back. And when the owner dies, it'll be resentful. No, just take it back with you.

My mother halted at the school gate and looked around, taking it in as if she had come to purchase the school grounds. Then she headed toward the main building so briskly I could hardly keep up. She opened the door to the staff room and pushed me in ahead of her, then followed and stood glowering. Just then my homeroom teacher arrived. He had cerebral palsy and couldn't use his right arm and leg easily, but he was kind to his students.

My mother greeted the teacher, then abruptly poked me in the side. "What are you waiting for? Say hello to your teacher."

I made my usual small bow. When my mother pinched my cheek, I said, "Ouch!"

"Did you see that? He's finally talking."

Her loud, sharp voice echoed across the room. My fierce shame amplified my mother's actions and voice to the tenth power. I was humiliated and wanted to die right there on the spot. She was so ecstatic that she seemed to want to show off to the idiots (she later lumped everyone in the staff room as idiots) that her son was normal. She wanted to be compensated for all her suffering. I knew too well what the teachers' cool, sour faces meant as they looked at my mother. Like the crazy evangelizers on the subway, my mother wasn't paying any attention to how the others felt as she threw a fit in the peaceful office. My homeroom teacher uncomfortably stammered out something at me.

It was the first time I'd heard his voice, since we had always used sign language in the classroom.

"Donggyu, are you able to speak now? Yes?"

Before I could answer, my mother cut in and said, "I'm telling you, he does."

But my teacher continued gazing at me. I could definitely speak. But if I spoke, I would be banished from the class, and if I didn't, my mother would stay put in the staff room and continue torturing me. My mother grabbed me by the shoulder and my teacher knelt (a difficult position for him) and looked into my eyes. I wasn't sure what to do, so I looked everywhere but at him. My mother's high heels kept up their nervous tapping. Finally, shame won over fear. I wanted to get my mother out so I said, "Yes, teacher."

"That's wonderful. Why don't you say one more thing?"

"I'm sorry."

My mother interrupted again. "Sorry? What on earth are you sorry for?"

Like an archer in ancient Greece wielding a large bow, my homeroom teacher thrust out one leg and used that tension to heave himself up. Then after patting me on the head, he returned to his desk and filled out my transfer documents. My mother must have keenly anticipated congratulations and praise because, once disappointed, she began subtly attacking the staff, suggesting that a perfectly normal child had attended a special needs program due to the school's mistake. My teacher silently withstood the criticism, adding only one thing: "Isn't it a relief that he can speak now?"

My teacher signed all the necessary documents, inserted them into an official school envelope, and handed it over. My mother removed the documents and returned the envelope to him. I wanted to say farewell to my classmates, who were always warm and gentle, friends who were nearly all dumb, but my teacher didn't allow it.

He said, "With your mother here, I think it's best that you return home today. Why don't you visit another time?"

I felt as if I'd been targeted and banished. At the school gate, my mother halted and spit in the school's direction, as if protecting herself from the source of a life-threatening infectious disease.

The first day at the regular school, I covered my ears to endure the clamor around me. Recess felt like torture. The kids shrieked like cicadas. Seeing me with my ears covered, they surrounded me one by one. They began poking me the way you would a dog in a pet store's display window; they were curious about what kinds of sounds a donkey who'd transferred from a special needs school would make. Instead of answering, I punched wildly at them. A kid I hit lost a front tooth and began crying, so a teacher rushed over and soothed him, saying, "Don't cry, it's okay, you'll grow a new one." She then lifted me up and isolated me from the others.

"Why did you hit him?" she kept asking.

I clammed up.

My teacher leaned in close and said, "If you keep acting like this, you'll be sent back to the special needs school."

That was exactly what I wanted, so I clung to my silence. But my silent protest ended when my swollen-eyed mother and my grandmother showed up at school.

When I went outside at recess, I ran into Jae.

"So you're talking now?"

"Yeah."

"You seem like a different kid."

"No, it's still me."

Jae's eyes narrowed as he studied me. He said, "Let's walk home together."

"Okay."

"Something's off." Jae stared at my lips.

"Why?"

"I feel like you're speaking in English," he said, "and I'm understanding what you're saying."

6

JUST AFTER I BEGAN TALKING, MY FATHER AND
mother separated. It was a coincidence, but from a kid's point
of view, it was clear everything started going wrong because of
me. One night when I went into the living room, I saw my uncle
down on his knees. My father was sitting on the sofa tight-lipped
with his eyes fixed to the TV. After kneeling on his numb legs
like that for over an hour, my uncle dragged himself out of the
house. I never saw him at our place again, not even on holidays
or at ancestral ceremonies. My mother returned to her family's
home in Busan. I began hearing the word "divorce" a lot inside
and outside the house.

After the Guam accident, Mama Pig drifted from restaurant to restaurant; it was right after the Asian Financial Crisis in
1997, so work was erratic. She began drinking *soju* every night.
Her snack of choice was raw garlic dipped in spicy pepper paste,
and Jae had to learn how to cook hangover stew. After waking
up early and pan-frying dried pollock to make a soup, he woke
Mama Pig, made sure she ate, then went to school. Whenever
she was drunk she sat Jae down and told him how she had taken
him from a bathroom in the Seoul Express Bus Terminal.

"I'm sorry," she said. "If I hadn't done that, you'd be somewhere better."

Jae didn't believe her, since she told that story only when

drunk. But after repeated retellings, he started to wonder if the story was actually true.

The city began redeveloping our neighborhood into apartment complexes. The residents formed an association, people diligently made rounds collecting signatures, and hung signs. Shouting broke out from the neighborhood's alleys and fights happened every day. Our once peaceful neighborhood turned into a chaos of factions. Even kids took sides. Kids whose families were homeowners and kids whose families rented stopped playing together. Homeowners received substantial compensation and the option to move into the newly built apartment complex, and renters didn't, so they faced dramatically different circumstances. We owned our house, but because we had invested a lot of money in remodeling it into a multi-unit, we would have very little cash after we returned the renters' deposits. Jae's situation was even worse. After full-scale relocation started, renters like his family would receive next to nothing and be forced out.

When we entered the fourth grade, Jae and I ended up in different classes. As usual, my father rarely returned home. At first one of my aunts came by and helped with the housekeeping, but over time she rarely visited. Mama Pig continued drinking. As the number of Chinese-Korean migrant workers increased, restaurant work became even scarcer. Mama Pig began living with a younger man whom we called Meth Head; widespread rumors of his meth addiction followed him. He was an instructor at a driving school and didn't even seem to care about the World Cup. When Jae was watching a match in the living room, Meth Head walked past, somehow unaware that the Korean team had made it to the quarterfinals. Mama Pig was no different. Both would walk past Jae, enter and lock their bedroom door, not emerging until well into the night. Sometimes their door stayed locked till morning. Jae skipped meals more often than he ate, and regularly went to school without proper supplies. At some point Meth Head stopped going to the driving school and stayed cooped up at home. They were clearly surviving on whatever income Mama Pig earned.

As for us, our family left the neighborhood. Now that we attended different classes and lived in different houses, Jae and I grew apart. While the rest of the world was going wild about the Korean soccer team making it to the semifinals, Jae lived day to day, feeling as if he were holding up a massive coffin lid by himself. The teachers found Jae disagreeable since he came without the required school supplies, and the other kids ignored him. Still, school was better than home. He couldn't breathe at home. Not knowing what to do, he'd hover outside his mother's locked bedroom door, the symbol of complete rejection. Mama Pig's gasping carried through the walls. He was old enough now to know exactly what weird act had played out between Popeye and the witch in the liquor storage. When he was hungry, he thought about the hostess club's bountiful kitchen. And he began to suspect that the story Mama Pig told him whenever she was drunk might actually be true.

7

SOON AFTER JAE ENTERED MIDDLE SCHOOL, HIS homeroom teacher called me in. His hobby was photography and he sometimes entered his work in amateur photo exhibits, half-forcing the students to attend. We had to write reports about our thoughts on his photos of a heron perched in white rapids and homeless people in a drunken stupor. The teacher was nicknamed "Bald Eagle" for his baldness, as well as "the bald homo," but I don't know if he was actually gay.

When he asked me if I knew why Jae had been absent for more than a few days, I realized that I hadn't seen Jae at school for some time.

"I don't know. We're in different classes and different neighborhoods now. I haven't seen him for a while."

Bald Eagle looked at the computer. "But you two have the same address."

"Teacher, that's an old address. We moved."

"Does Jae still live there?"

"I think so, probably."

He twirled his pen and muttered to himself, "Can people still live there?"

\\\\\\\\\\\\

I shouldered my way past the cram-school shuttle buses at the school gate that snatched up each kid who exited, and headed toward our old house. I followed a line of well-built structures along a narrow back road until I came to a six-lane street. The neighborhood was surrounded by a makeshift two-meter-high barricade, but there seemed to be no real effort to hide it. The dirty, battered fence was merely a sign that the neighborhood would be demolished soon, and until a decent apartment complex was constructed in its place, this was a useless, temporary landscape.

Jae could be somewhere inside those barriers. I debated several times whether to turn back. Honestly, I really didn't want to have anything to do with him anymore. I now had friends in middle school who lived in my apartment complex and went to the same cram schools. They were ordinary kids, and I could have ordinary friendships with them. We laughed and talked as we flipped through comic books, or formed teams and played computer games. That complicated life with Jae was behind me. But deep down, a part of me knew I owed him. I hadn't forgotten that back when everyone ignored me, Jae had stuck by me.

I took the crosswalk and headed to where I thought Jae might be. Each empty house had a big red X scrawled in paint across its doors, which meant the house could be demolished. Some roofs had already caved in; I saw a dirty teddy bear missing its eyes and Barbie dolls with broken necks, scattered. The redevelopment association and the construction firm had put up signs between the telephone poles. In the deteriorating neighborhood, those new signs gleamed with messages written on white backgrounds:

WE WELCOME THE BEGINNING OF RELOCATION AND HAPPI-
NESS IS JUST AHEAD OF US. What they actually meant: "Please
cooperate and leave quickly so the new apartment complex can
be built. Then we'll be one day closer to moving into proper
homes." Someone had handwritten BULLSHIT in red marker.
Beside that someone else had scrawled FOOL, GO AHEAD AND
SPEND THE REST OF YOUR LIFE POOR.

I felt suspicious gazes coming from some of the still-occupied
houses. Peering out from the dark, and seeing that the visitor was
only a middle school student, they relaxed and receded back
into the shadows. Wherever full-scale redevelopment began, no
one bothered to repair or rebuild their houses, so the streets resembled an old photograph. The contours were familiar, but the
neighborhood's faded appearance felt alien. It reminded me of
strange streets from my nightmares or from historical sets in doc-
umentaries meant to replicate the Goryeo and Joseon periods.

Before I knew it, I arrived at the house where I'd been born
and raised. A red X was slashed across the rusted steel gate. It
reminded me of a biblical story I'd learned when I briefly went
to church. The story told of the Israelites, a chosen people who
saved their children by marking their front doors before a wrath-
ful angel came to kill their enemies' children.

I opened the gate, walked into the yard, and saw in the flow-
erbed a toy car missing its wheels that I'd played with as a kid.
There was no sign of life; I suddenly felt scared. There wasn't a
single person around and even if I screamed, I was sure no one
would show up. I would have fled if it hadn't been my house. I
worked up the courage to go to the second floor where Jae's family had lived. The stairs were much narrower and more dangerous than I remembered, and there was no noise coming from

inside. I cautiously tugged at the doorknob. It didn't open; it was firmly locked.

"Jae."

No one responded.

"Are you inside? It's me, Donggyu."

I rang the bell and knocked but as expected, no one answered. This hideous-looking neighborhood with its oppressive silence pulled me back into the trauma of aphonia. You could call aphonia a mental form of claustrophobia. It's a feeling as if my heart were a black hole sucking my words back into me. The gravitational pull was so strong, it had seemed impossible to send anything outward. The memory alone was suffocating. I ran back down the stairs. It wasn't like I had an obligation to find Jae. I raced down to the first floor and headed toward the gate, but someone grabbed me by the waist of my pants and pulled me back. I lost my balance and tottered, then was dragged in.

"Keep quiet."

Jae didn't bring me to his apartment, but to the semi-basement unit that Pakistani family had once rented. Jae shoved me inside, scoped out our surroundings, and then closed the door.

He said, "You came alone?"

"Why're you acting like this?"

"Who sent you?"

"Your homeroom teacher."

He relaxed but he also seemed somehow disappointed. After my eyes adjusted to the dark, I looked around carefully. Compared to the mess outside, the house was surprisingly tidy.

"Why're you here, and not in your family's place?"

"There's no such thing as *my place* here. You can live anywhere in this neighborhood now."

"It'll be demolished soon."

"True."

"Is your mother out?"

Jae's face went blank. His eyes closed and his neck jerked back, and he looked excruciatingly bored; he did this whenever he was furious.

"What's that?" I pointed at two full-length mirrors standing behind him. The mirrors were upright and facing each other so that within one mirror there was a mirror, and within that another mirror, and within that mirror yet another mirror, endlessly multiplying themselves.

"I found them. A lot of people get rid of their mirrors when they move."

He dodged the point of my question. I wondered why he had two mirrors facing each other, but he changed the subject. "You remember Meth Head?"

"Of course I remember him."

Even before we'd moved, Jae's face had been purple with bruises. Meth Head had beat him up, but Mama Pig was so high that she didn't care what happened to Jae. Everyone was shocked at how the tough, determined Mama Pig had fallen apart in the blink of an eye, but no one called the police or reported the beatings. I wondered if maybe Meth Head and Mama Pig were still on the second floor and left Jae alone in the semi-basement.

As if he had read my mind, Jae said, "I found the house clean after coming back from school one day. Since those two started using meth, the house was always a mess. I thought it was weird, and when it got dark, no one returned home."

"When was that?"

"About a month ago."

"You've been living alone here a whole month?" I thought, In these spooky ruins?

"I have to find the bastard."

"And when you find him?"

"I'll get even."

"Get even?"

His eyes flashed a flaming blue.

"You see what it's like here now, don't you? If anything happens to someone, no one will know."

"What about reporting them to the police?"

Jae smirked. "First thing they'll do is lock me up in an orphanage."

A stepmother who'd abandoned her child and made a run for it wouldn't be worth a minute's attention from the police; for women without money, applying for a divorce was a bother, and they just slipped out of the house and split.

"Do you know what this is?" Jae pointed at the mirrors set in the center of the room.

"No."

"It's a device to catch the devil. A kind of trap."

"It catches the devil?"

"I read about it in a book. The devil can move between mirrors if they're facing each other — he comes out to cross over to the other. If you cover the second mirror with a cloth just then, the devil can't finish crossing and ends up stuck here. That's when you grab him."

He sounded like a salesman talking about the features of the latest TV set. According to him, the devil was most active crossing between mirrors on Fridays at midnight.

"If he's so easily caught, how can he be the devil?"

"The devil doesn't know how he was captured. That's why if he wants to return to his world, he needs the help of the trap-maker."

"What in the world are you going to do after you catch the devil?" I found myself saying this seriously.

"Weren't you paying attention? I said I'm going to get even."

"Okay, but you can't keep living like this. Do you have food?"

"There's a lot of leftovers in the empty houses. People leave everything that's past the expiration date, so whenever a family moves out, I go over at night and clean the house out."

My guess was that he wasn't just hitting empty houses.

"You're not going to tell the school you saw me, right?"

"I won't say anything. But this area will be redeveloped soon anyway, and a bulldozer will raze it all down."

He nodded somberly. "That's why I have to find the devil, quick."

He showed me weird phrases that he had written down, and explained that they were commands for the devil that he had found on the Internet. He was utterly sincere.

I couldn't leave him like this, so I said, "I heard fires have been breaking out in the neighborhood."

There were a lot of wild rumors about the area. As one household left, then the next, the number of abandoned buildings grew. The association wasn't pleased about opponents to the redevelopment plans, and ignored the growing disorder in the area. In fact they encouraged it.

"You mean the random fires? They're started by the shits from the redevelopment association."

Jae was sure about this. He pointed at the stacks of dry-powder fire extinguishers beside the table, and said he'd collected them from the empty houses.

I added, "I even heard that someone kidnapped and killed a girl, and put her in a water tank."

"All kinds of rumors get around."

"Aren't you scared?"

Instead of answering, he pointed at the mirrors and grinned. There was nothing cheerful about his smile.

I stood up. "I skipped out on one cram school already tonight, so I've got to make it to the next one."

Jae went out first and scouted the surroundings like an advance guard, then let me go.

Jae still didn't show up at school. I lied to Bald Eagle and told him I hadn't been able to find Jae. Sometimes I packed food and brought it to the basement where he was hiding out. He didn't make much progress capturing the devil, but he said that something was definitely moving between the mirrors and he just hadn't caught it at the right moment. Like the alchemists who had spent their lives mixing different ingredients with lead in order to make gold, every Friday at midnight, Jae made small changes to his method. He made adjustments such as revising his commands, making microscopic shifts to the mirrors' angles, or lighting a candle between the two mirrors. If he failed, he had to wait another week. He hadn't cut his hair for a long time and it had gone shaggy, which made him look like a retired rocker.

"How long are you going to live like this?"

"Till I catch him."

Jae was stubborn. His cheeks had hollowed out and his arms were bones. Each time I opened his door and went in, I was afraid I'd discover his cold, stiff corpse.

8

ONE DAY DURING A LATE APRIL SNOW, I SOUGHT OUT
Bald Eagle. The snow stuck to the windows of the staff room in
random patterns before quickly melting.

I asked, "If, let's say, Jae was living alone without any grownups taking care of him, what would happen to him? Would he
be sent to an orphanage?"

"So you saw Jae?" Bald Eagle said, picking his ear.

"No, sir, I'm just asking. I'm just curious what would happen."

"Have you seen Jae, or haven't you?"

"Do I have to tell you?"

His eyes narrowed. "No, you don't have to say anything. But
if Jae is living alone in that neighborhood — as you would know
since you've been there — it's very dangerous. He'd have to be
taken somewhere safe. For his sake."

"Even if he didn't want to go?"

"If he didn't want to go, we'd have to find another solution.
This is a democracy, after all."

A few days later when I went to meet Jae, I was being followed. I had no idea until I strode over to the basement room
and knocked. As soon as Jae opened the door, the police, a social
worker, and redevelopment association board members shoved
me away and flooded the room. Jae, sprawled across the floor in
front of me, was dragged out like a dog. He struggled, but they

were too much for him. He glared at me, his eyes filled with resentment. I still remember what he said as he clung to the rusted doorknob: "Just give me one more day! Today's Friday the thirteenth!"

Only I understood what he meant. As the police officer unlocked the door to the car, Jae used all his strength to shake off his captors and escape. He dashed up to the multi-unit's rooftop and leaped from roof to roof, balcony to balcony. He moved easily, as if he had done this often. It looked like he could run forever. Everyone separated and began combing the area.

I went to Jae's room and stood between the two mirrors. I saw countless copies of myself. What if Jae hadn't been trying to catch the devil and had wanted to enter the mirror instead? Or what if he'd given a part or all of his soul to that other world? When I consider his life from that point onward, it seems to me that the moment he had stood between the two mirrors, he broke away from the rules and the ways of the world that had twice abandoned him and entered a different, eternal sphere. Jae didn't really need to capture the devil leaping between the mirrors. The only object reflected in a mirror is the self; and a person who persists in continuously gazing at himself is actually looking at the devil.

The next day, Bald Eagle summoned me. He said that they had caught Jae and sent him to a facility. This was a good thing in all respects, he explained, and he praised me for having done something difficult for my friend's sake.

"Where did they get him?"

"They say he returned to the house. One of the board members staking it out caught him."

Within the next month, bulldozers razed the area. The last resistance came from the elderly and the sick, those without money, power, or mobility. As the machines advanced, 119 rescue workers drove in and carried people out on stretchers. Within days, they buried the memories of all the former residents in the red flatland that now resembled Mars. A construction company erected a temporary barricade decorated with appealing photos around the area. The apartment was branded something like Dream&Green, or maybe it was e-Convenient World. My memory's shaky.

Despite rumors, no middle school female's corpse turned up in the water tank. The construction firm wasn't actually worried about a decaying corpse but about what didn't decay — the remains of ancient kingdoms. Construction halted if a worker discovered a thousand-year-old fragment of a tiled roof or the smallest trace of a fortress wall from the Three Kingdoms.

That winter, I sent Jae a Christmas card. Bald Eagle gave me the address after he made a few calls to some bureau of education and learned which facility Jae had been shipped off to. I remember thinking that for grownups, everything was so simple.

"Where is Nonsan-ri?" I asked.

"It's near Daejeon."

It was less than a two-hour drive away, but to a middle school kid like me, Daejeon might as well have been another country.

I had wanted to visit Jae, but Bald Eagle said, "Maybe just send him a card."

There was something offensive about the way he phrased it.

He didn't say "Why don't you send him a card" or "You should send him a card" or "How about sending him a card?" Instead, he said, "Maybe just send him a card." His flippant tone tainted my innocent plan, but it was also an idea that hadn't occurred to me. By then I owned a cell phone; but Jae had never had one before and there was even less of a chance now, with him in a facility in Nonsan-ri.

At a stationery store near school, I bought a card picturing Rudolph dancing. Inside there was hardly any space for writing, but I needed to clear up any misunderstandings, ask Jae how he was, and tell him how I was. There just wasn't enough space for all I needed to say. Oh, whatever, I thought, and started writing. I ended up with a typical Christmas greeting. How are you? I'm doing well. How is it there? Merry Christmas.

Looking back, I can see that Jae probably felt I was taunting him. It was obvious he would think I'd told the school everything and landed him in the facility, and then had the nerve to send him a Christmas card casually asking him how it was there, and wishing him a merry Christmas! But a small part of me hoped that no matter what I wrote, he would understand me. After all, hadn't he been my interpreter when I couldn't speak for myself?

I went to the post office and mailed the card, then headed to the Gwanghwamun district. After buying some study guides at a bookstore I headed home on the subway, where I ran into a group of deaf people. Five kids around my age were using sign language together. I'd forgotten a lot, but I still got the gist of what they were saying. Four of them mercilessly teased the fifth, signing: *You're dating her, aren't you? There're rumors all over school.* The kid being teased fought back: *Who knows, maybe she's got a crush on me, but that's her problem!* The kids shook their heads and laughed. They abruptly began talking about movies. They must have just come from watching a foreign-language comedy that they couldn't hear, but they would have read the subtitles like anyone else. Though it was quiet and only their expressions hinted at laughter, I'm sure everyone on the train sensed elation surging from the group. The kids mimicked the actors' expressions and jabbered on about the movie's climax. The other passengers had no idea how many words were flooding out of them.

If they would only accept me, I wanted to be a part of them again. But if there's a sadness that inflames the heart, a sadness akin to resentment and grief, there also exists a judge, a cousin to sadness, who chills it. That day I felt the latter, as if my heart had frosted over with snow. My eyes prickled with pain as my heart went cold. I turned up the volume on my MP3 player. The kids got off at the next subway station, and birds — their wings flapping — rose up from their hands.

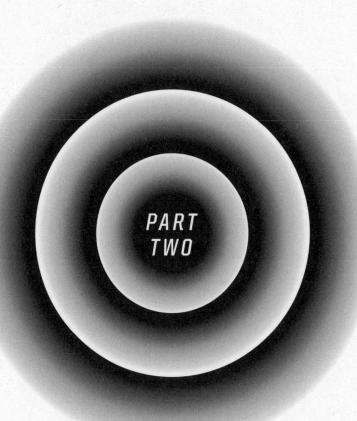

PART
TWO

9

A DOG-BREEDING FARM STOOD BEHIND THE OR-
phanage. The owner had sold his cows after their value collapsed, and bought dogs instead. Though he crammed hundreds of dogs into the small fenced-in area, the dogs stayed quiet
because he had punctured each of their eardrums with an air
gun. It's said that if you shoot an unloaded gun into a dog's ear,
the penetrating air tears the dog's eardrum. The dog breeder
drove a truck. Sometimes he stopped by to meet the director of
the orphanage. He looked at children the same way he looked
at dogs, so the kids instinctively avoided him. Once a girl disappeared, and everyone suspected the dog breeder. Rumors spread
that he had killed her and fed her to the dogs.

A mushroom grower, the dog breeder's sworn enemy, lived
behind the breeding farm. He grew mushrooms in an abandoned mine that Jae had once sneaked inside, along with a few
other kids. It was dark and damp and sent chills up the spine.
The smooth white mushrooms spiraled bleakly up thick blocks
of wood. When one of the kids claimed that all the mushrooms
were poisonous, they started arguing.

Jae protested, "Why would he spend money growing poisonous mushrooms?"

The other kid picked a mushroom off the wood and handed
it to him. He said, "It's because the owner's totally psychotic. Eat

it, asshole. What, you won't scarf it down? You said it wasn't poisonous, didn't you?"

Jae stared blankly at the mushroom, then handed it back. "You eat it."

"Why should I eat it? You said it wasn't poisonous, so you should eat it."

Jae said, "Now I think they're poisonous too."

"What?"

"Now that I think about it, I think you're right. It is a poisonous mushroom. It's poisonous, all right."

The kid, confused by Jae's sudden reversal, stared at him. Jae held the mushroom close to the kid's nose. He said, "Here, I said try it. What's the matter? You can't eat it since it's poisonous?"

The kid stepped back, shouting, "Asshole, are you crazy? Why should I eat it?"

"Try it, asshole. What, you scared?" Jae brought the mushroom to his own lips. "Watch carefully. This is how you eat a poisonous mushroom."

In front of all the kids, Jae chewed it thoroughly and swallowed. But though the mushroom wasn't poisonous, Jae was still racked with diarrhea all night long.

The mushroom grower had put up a hut where he lived right beside the damp tunnel sheltering a variety of mushrooms. Prostitutes from the coffeehouse sometimes came by, so the older boys peeked in through the window. The man lived with a twenty-four-hour news channel on at all times, so the news became the background noise even when he was having sex with these young women. The prostitute's mechanical, insincere moans rode over the anchorwoman's serious voice mostly relaying what politicians were doing. Whenever the couple finished having sex, they poured coffee from a thermos and drank it together in silence.

The coffeehouse girls always arrived on scooters with weak engines. And when they departed, they left behind smoky exhaust from the burning engines and the scent of cheap perfume. Both were toxic, but this illicit smell captivated Jae early on. Sometimes he followed it down the road, but the scent was inevitably masked by the time he arrived at the dog-breeding farm. From there, the world of dogs took over. The whole area reeked of dog shit and urine. When the owner wasn't around, Jae sneaked into the farm. Each time the tense dogs, raised for fighting, came at the fence as if to tear it apart, Jae backed off. They stank with the smell of creatures living a dire, doomed existence. He felt strongly sympathetic toward the trapped dogs, and was especially taken with a red-eyed Tosa Inu who limped because of a bad hind leg. For a time the two merely gazed at each other as if in a staring contest, and whenever that happened, even the other dogs calmed down.

You could say that Jae had a rare ability to communicate with animals, but he had trouble talking to people while he lived at the orphanage. People who met Jae for the first time, especially girls, were interested in him, but it didn't last long. He didn't know how to hold a person's attention, but he was surprisingly able to make deep connections with animals. And the more this happened, the less he expected of people.

The coffeehouse girls stopped by the dog-breeding farm,

though not as frequently as they did at the mushroom farm. Some days they visited the mushroom farm first, and sometimes the other way around. When the girls went to the dog farm, the kids didn't follow and peek in. They were terrified of the rumors that if caught, they would be fed to the dogs and disappear without a trace. Only Jae was fearless.

One day Jae ran into a coffeehouse girl coming down from the mushroom farm. She poured leftover coffee from the thermos and handed it to him.

She said, "So you're here again."

Jae got ready to flee from her and the red blouse revealing the hollow between her breasts. The young woman must have read his mind because she lightly took his arm. "Do you want a cookie? This isn't for the customers — it's mine. Here, have it. It's delicious."

He ate the cookie. In high heels, the woman was much taller than him. This moment, in which he accepted the coffee and then the cookie from her with both hands, would have the significance of a spiritual awakening for him.

"Do you want to see a movie with me sometime?" she asked.

Jae only finished swallowing the cookie and fled down the hill.

10

JAE DREW A MAP OF HIS WORLD WHEN HIS ENTIRE
universe was the small mountain and the orphanage. A tiny village where young children lived sat at the foot of the hill. Above perched a kingdom where an evil monarch ruled over fierce dogs, and at the highest point, nestled in a deep cave, fairies made a mushroom their house. Far from those concentric circles, he drew a castle with blooming flowers — basically, the home he'd left behind — that looked like the utopia the ancients had dreamed of. Ever since he was young, Jae's view of the world was truly his own. He wasn't interested in what schools taught. Instead he saw with his own eyes and rarely believed anything that grownups said. For instance, he quickly figured out that the idea of democracy taught at school was a sham. He understood too well the fate of dogs allotted equal amounts of space and fed the same meals but that were still trapped, unable to take a single step out of the pen.

The fire began some fifty meters up from the dog pen, meaning that it started in the bushy slope leading to the mushroom farm. At first the wind blew from the foot of the mountain so the flames burned the withered bushes and spread uphill. By the time the orphans woke to "Fire!" and stared up at the mountain from the yard, it was still dark and the crimson flames seemed about to swallow up the mushrooms. Suddenly the wind halted and a strange silence fell. But only for a moment, before a violent wind blew downward and changed direction. The dogs, catching the scent of stinging smoke, began whining even more wildly. There was no sign of a fire truck, and the orphanage's employees and the kids simply watched from afar.

Jae ran toward the dog farm, leading a few curious kids who waved sticks in the air. Embers danced like fireflies. Jae nearly ran into the farm owner dashing down the mountain as he flailed his arms and ran like a lunatic. One of the kids, overwhelmed with fright, reversed direction and ran down after him. Jae and two remaining kids entered the dog farm, which was in flames, and flung open the dog pen. The dogs, smelling death, forgot their own fierce nature and tore out of the kennel with their tails tucked in. A few lacked the courage to leave the kennel and huddled in the corner, trembling. Embers the size of summer flies had grown into fist-sized balls of flame flaring through the sky.

"Get out now!" Jae said. "You stupid mutts!"

The dogs didn't budge, so he lit an old newspaper and hurled it into the pen. Only then did the dogs cautiously emerge and begin running, their butts smeared with dried shit. Jae ran downhill after them. The dogs climbed onto boulders with good views of the area, gazed back at the farm that the hungry fire had devoured, and whimpered. With large dogs appearing and disappearing on all sides and the blazing flames and stinging smoke, the landscape resembled the pictures of hell that hang in Buddhist temples. Fire trucks, late to the scene, wove up the crooked roads, perilously making their way toward the dog-breeding farm. Jae arrived at the orphanage with his face blackened by smoke, but only after the others had taken shelter farther down the mountain. He waited in the yard for everyone to return.

Once the fire was under control, the others came back. The older students told Jae that the dog breeder had been in an accident. He'd been running madly down the hill when a milk delivery truck hit him. Next they said that two bodies untouched by the fire were discovered at the mushroom farm. Someone had stabbed the farmer with a sharp knife and strangled the coffeehouse woman beside him. The police officer who arrived at the orphanage said the two had clearly been attacked in their sleep and the murderer had started a fire to destroy the evidence. But, because of the shifting wind, the cover-up hadn't gone as planned. That was when the orphanage director informed the police about the long-standing grudge between the dog breeder and the mushroom farmer.

11

WHILE THE POLICE SEARCHED THE MUSHROOM farmer's residence, trucks pulled up into the empty lot across from the orphanage. Men carrying snares emerged from them and climbed up the mountain.

"They're here to catch the dogs," said a guy two years older than Jae, as he spit on the floor, his eyes bright with excitement.

Once the hunt began, the men snared the calf-size dogs that had simultaneously tasted fear and freedom, and dragged them back to lock them up one at a time in wire cages. The men strained their eyes as they combed the smoky mountain for the sight of one more dog. The dogs were either hiding near the in-tact mushroom farm or had crossed the mountain toward a village near the cement factory. More trucks were waiting for the dogs there.

Jae found a sharp nail, approached the trucks where the trapped dogs waited alone, and slashed the tires. They made a *woosh woosh* sound as the trucks slowly sank. The dogs, remembering Jae's scent, stopped barking and whimpered instead. Red Eyes was among them. With his limp, he'd be the first one sold for meat. As Jae punctured the tires of a fifth truck, a fist struck his head like lightning from behind and stunned him. The three dog hunters dragged him to the orphanage director's office, but Jae was too weak to fight. They'd even lassoed him around the neck with a snare.

The three, officially dog breeders by profession, burst in while the director was watching television. His gaze landed on the snare around Jae's neck.

He asked the dog breeders, "What do you have there?"

"This brat, he's yours, right?" one of the dog breeders asked, looking a little timid.

As soon as the director nodded, they explained what had happened. Before they were finished, the director interrupted: "Can't you remove the damn noose?"

One of the dog breeders snatched the snare off Jae's neck. The director continued speaking. "It's a real pity, what happened, but the orphanage cannot be responsible for a student's misdeeds, and that's all I will say. If you're angry, feel free to bring him to the police and take the matter to court."

An elderly dog breeder stepped forward with his arms crossed. "Look here, Mr. Director. Do you think we can buy a single tire with the money from selling even one bitch? But this goddamn fucking son of a bitch here ruined twenty tires, tore them all up so we can't even patch them. I'm talking about this orphaned piece of shit here."

The dog breeder smacked Jae across the head. His small body flew and hit the wall. Jae struggled to stand.

"You know why I slashed the tires?"

The one who had smacked him said, "Oh, check out this asshole. Okay, so why'd you rip them up? Why don't you tell us, so I can rip your trap right off your face?" He rolled up his sleeves.

"Dogs have souls too. They have souls!" Jae's voice cracked.

One dog breeder responded, "They have souls. So what?"

All of them stepped forward in sync. They looked as if they

might, if needed, trample over Jae with their work boots. But he didn't back down.

He stared at them and said grimly, "I mean, you can't treat something with a soul that way."

"This runt, this little asshole, keeps talking to us like this, showing us no respect."

As they charged toward him, the director slapped the desk. He frowned and tapped cigarette ashes into an ashtray. "Let's put a stop to this. There's no point in arguing with the kid. He's an orphan, a bastard. There's no one to officially claim responsibility for what he's done. You see what I'm saying?"

Dealt a death blow, the men brooded over this reality. Just then an investigator coming from the mushroom farm stopped by the office for a cup of coffee, with a cop accompanying him.

The dog breeders, guilty of illegally hunting the homeless dogs, tried to sneak quietly out of the director's office, but the investigator called them back.

"You there, what is it you do for a living?" He spoke strangely, mixing informal and formal terms.

The director answered for them. "They're dog breeders."

The investigator slurped his coffee. "What brings dog breeders to an orphanage? Planning to adopt people instead of dogs?"

A dog breeder in a black down jacket said in protest, "That bastard slashed our tires."

The investigator turned his attention to Jae. "You, how old are you?"

"I'm fourteen."

"What's a little bastard like you puncturing people's car tires for?"

Jae didn't respond. The cop said to the dog breeders, "You

should really leave. It's not like he has parents to compensate you."

"What about the orphanage or this supervisor — isn't there any sense of responsibility here?" The man in the black jacket didn't back off. "I mean, this is an act of terrorism!"

The cop finally became annoyed. "I tried to explain the situation nicely to you people, but you clearly don't know your limits. Why don't we all go and officially file this case and investigate the details? Will the dog-breeder gentlemen here be able to receive compensation for their tires or not? What? Terrorism? If this is terrorism, then shiiiit, report it to the Americans and their FBI."

The dog breeders exchanged glances. They didn't like government institutions or the law since their way of life lay just at its boundaries — and maybe outside it. People often said that they secretly caught dogs that had owners, and — whether they turned them into fighting dogs or used them for meat — all their actions verged on illegal. The dog breeders standing near the door quietly slipped out one at a time.

The director helped Jae to his feet; he had collapsed again. "Jae, my boy, why did you rip up their tires? Why don't you tell me?"

"They have souls."

"Dogs don't have souls. Only people have souls."

"How do you know that?"

"The fact that humans are capable of sin is proof in itself that they have souls." The director sounded like he was justifying as he continued. "Dogs don't sin. They aren't able to commit a sin. Sinning, suffering, asking for forgiveness, and receiving salvation — this is what makes us human."

Jae responded, "Sin, doing wrong, people, animals. Dividing everything up like this is exactly what makes us human. We think we're high and mighty. I'm a human being. I'm at the very top. I know sin. Animals don't. That's why we can kill animals. That's your logic?"

The director straightened. "So you're saying what you did was right? But didn't you harm others? That's the same as stealing. Don't you agree?"

"There's something worse than stealing."

"What's that?"

"It's ignoring pain. It's not doing anything about someone's cries. The world of sin begins there."

"You can't avoid pain."

"You can't avoid it, but you can try. You shouldn't inflict unnecessary pain on humans or animals for your own benefit."

"It would be great if everything were as simple as you make it."

"What's so complicated about it?"

"Then who decides whose suffering is more important? You? You think only the dogs trapped in cages suffer? Those dog breeders work hard at making ends meet, and they have families too. Their kids might have to go without food for a day because you slashed their tires."

"But if we pick everything apart like that, we won't ever get anything done."

"You need to grow up first, then maybe you'll understand that the world's not that simple."

"If I can't make decisions now, it won't change when I grow up. I acted based on how I saw it. I don't have any regrets."

"You hold a grudge against the world. That's why you want to judge it with your petty version of justice. That's dangerous."

Jae nodded seriously as if he were a consumer listening to instructions on how to use an electrical appliance. "Yes, it is dangerous," he said. "I know that too."

12

JAE ENDED UP WITH A WEEK OF SOLITARY CONFINE-
ment. The room chosen to punish the orphans received hardly
any light, and instead of a bathroom, there was a bowl. Books
weren't allowed, so all you had was the sound of your own
breathing.

A strong feeling rising up in Jae's body confused him, and
only after two dark days alone did he realize it was rage. One
hundred percent pure rage. Its hot toxicity burned through him
like sulfuric acid. His stomach acted up so he couldn't digest
anything he swallowed, and he threw up on the plates he was
eating from. He began avoiding food. After a day or two the
vomit dried and stopped giving off a smell. During the long,
lonely nights on an empty stomach, he entered the next stage.
This differed from the meditation practice of monks and yogis.
It was more like being possessed — his soul entered and occu-
pied other lives, then inhabited them as if they were his own.

One time, he located Red Eyes, whom he had freed. The
dog had eluded the hunters and was still roaming across the
hills. Jae entered Red Eyes' soul, saw the world through his eyes,
felt the hunger signals sent by the dog's stomach, and detected
the atmosphere of fear that the dog's sensitive ears picked up.
Red Eyes repeatedly dreamed about escaping the depths of an
abandoned mine, then going through the stinging smoke. He
dreamed of dogfights in which he tore at another dog's ear. But

outside of those nightmarish moments, Red Eyes' soul was surprisingly peaceful. He could endure an eternity of time just resting his head on his front paws.

Then, as if someone had pulled a plug, Jae felt his soul sucked out of the Tosa Inu. He thought he might be losing his mind. But without any contact with other souls, he couldn't endure the sharp teeth of the eternal darkness, and like a hacker who finds a lapse in security and infiltrates a system, whenever Jae caught a soul off guard he quickly entered it.

The coffeehouse girl's abandoned scooter was blackened by flames and coated with mold-like fire-extinguishing foam. Even after the fire trucks left, the scooter kept releasing black smoke from its burning tires. Jae stayed inside the scooter for a while. He heard innumerable voices murmuring there, as if it were a haunted house in an amusement park. The inner world of the Tosa Inu was peaceful, but the scooter kept up a racket like an out-of-control manic patient. He wasn't sure whether the voice belonged to the scooter, the woman who had ridden it, or even another soul who had entered it and was bemoaning his fate, but for some reason, Jae was fond of the scooter. He sensed its dynamic, self-assured spirit indifferent to its environment.

"I'll tell you what it's like to ride a scooter and race." The voice was playful. "It's like a yo-yo. The road enters the scooter's soul, then reemerges. We don't actually race 'over' the road; you could say we reel it in, then let it go. The road isn't outside us — it's running through us."

In the middle of the endless babbling, Jae sensed a chilly soul silently enter and leave. He thought that it might be the scooter's last owner, the strangled girl. A girl with tattooed eyebrows and full lips. He recalled the taste of the cookie she'd given him. Though this had already happened, it felt like it was coming from the future. The concept of time didn't have much meaning for Jae, who was bound to a machine. The difference between the definite past and the unknown future blurred, and future events felt like past experiences, and memories of the past like ominous prophecies.

Suddenly a sharp noise and a burning light flooded the room, but Jae's eyes wouldn't open. Someone told him that his confinement was over. Like a drunk waking up in a strange location, Jae tried to regain his sense of reality. The chaos of time fell back into the right order with some difficulty, and his soul finally returned to his neglected body. He left solitary confinement, dragging his numb leg behind him. Just above his head two magpies squawked, then headed south.

13

JAE TOOK AN EXPRESS BUS TO SEOUL. WHEN IT
glided into the terminal, he felt a deep sense of peace, as if he
had returned to a place where he was meant to be. Hundreds
of buses releasing exhaust, the noise of diesel engines echoing off the ceilings, passengers crowding in from all directions,
the touts, fanatics, and peddlers — all of it comforted Jae's soul.
He stood alert in the center of the terminal's waiting room and
closed his eyes. Noises sprang at him and smells grew stronger.
He tried to picture a teenage girl only two years older than him,
walking into the terminal to give birth.

It wasn't easy. Instead of an image, he recalled a phrase:
"What's bound to happen will happen." As he was mulling it
over, his nerves heightened as if he were sharpening a knife. The
bus terminal began to resemble the uterus of an enormous monster. He wanted to penetrate the consciousness of the strange
building that had birthed him, but he couldn't find an entry
point or any clues. His consciousness drifted into the dusty atmosphere of the terminal; he couldn't go any deeper.

It might not be the right time, he thought.

As soon as he opened his eyes, the terminal rushed in as
though approaching him. Then two men bumped into him as
they passed.

\\\\\\\\\\\\

At age sixteen, Jae is now in Daehangno.

The streets are flooded with people who move steadily without taking much interest in their surroundings. They focus only on the brightly lit window displays and the crowds approaching from the opposite direction. Like robots equipped with delicate sensors, they head for their destination without bumping into one another. But if a person takes an interest in the environment — if he picks something up from the ground or stops and looks around — he disrupts the flow. In this case, most detour around the obstruction and rejoin the moving mass of people, forgetting the obstruction was ever there. But the homeless aren't like that. They are the streets' residents, so their interest lies in the streets themselves. They stay alert to everything happening around them. Just as a stray cat perched on a brick wall watches other stray cats, they recognize one another at once. Jae realized this immediately when he started his vagabond life.

In the Daehangno area Jae merged with the crowd and watched b-boys dancing onstage. The young dancers strained to demonstrate how high and brilliantly they could shoot up and defy gravity. The girls shouted in response to each pose, and their cheers came back in the form of even more extreme dance moves.

Jae had once dreamed about becoming a machine. In the dream he realized that he had to live on as a machine and accept this fate. For some reason he was unaware of it while it happened, but by the time he came to his senses, he had already become the machine. Maybe scenes from the movie *RoboCop* had influenced him. When he realized what had happened, he didn't feel unhappy and instead was impatient to test the machine's capabilities since he might be able to fly or break through a wall with one blow of his fist. But in the dream he wasn't able to move at all. When he was about to go mad from frustration, his body began moving with dizzying speed and mechanical regularity, but was still controllable. It moved to its own pattern.

As he watched the b-boys spinning on their heads like tops, he recalled the dream. It was as if elaborate mechanical parts made up their bodies. As if several machines he could watch but not control were getting tangled up in their dizzying movements. Jae felt helpless and stepped back, landing squarely on the foot of someone behind him.

Before he stepped on Mokran's foot, she had already noticed him. This boy was different, she must have thought, for he was wearing a fuzzy knit sweater and watching the dancers like a mathematician puzzling over a difficult formula. Like he might be gathering his strength to confront the explosive energy on the stage.

"It's okay," Mokran said when Jae apologized. She grabbed him as he tottered. "You feeling sick?"

Jae shook his head and looked up at her. As soon as she released his arm, he stumbled again, barely recovering his balance.

"How many days is it?"

"How many days of what?" At first he didn't understand her question.

"How many days is it since you left? I mean, since you left home."

It was three days, if the orphanage could be called home. But Jae didn't respond. Together they left the semicircle that had formed around the stage to sit on a bench in the shade of a ginkgo tree. Some drunken observers shouted as they passed. Mokran offered Jae a cigarette, which he accepted and lit.

"How many days is it for you?" Jae asked.

"Well, I just come and go."

"I'm Jae."

"Jae-hui? Isn't that a girl's name?"

"No, Jae. Not 'hui,' but 'ae,' as in 'two.'" Jae made a V sign at her with two fingers.

"What's your name?"

"Mokran."

"That's a strange name."

"You're one to talk!" Mokran giggled. "My dad, he thinks he's hot shit. I guess he wanted to stand out."

Her last name was Yeom. Yeom Mokran. It definitely wasn't a common name for girls these days.

He said, "It sounds like a name out of a textbook. A name of an independence movement leader."

"It's the national flower of North Korea."

"Your father named you after North Korea's national flower?"

"Yeah. My birthday's July sixth, and that day there just happened to be an article in the paper about North Korea's national flower. Something about how the *mokran* was the flower that Kim Il Sung first discovered. My dad has a soft spot for the North. He's probably still in Pyongyang."

"Is he in politics or something?"

"No, he's in the movie business. I heard he's directing TV commercials in the North these days."

Mokran rattled off some titles of movies that her father had produced. Even Jae had heard of one of them.

"It's fucking embarrassing." She drew on the ground with the toe of her shoe.

She told him about her father — an incurable skirt-chaser. Even after three marriages, he couldn't manage without a mistress. Mokran's mother was his second wife; Mokran had four brothers with different mothers. Her own mother had remarried and was living elsewhere, so Mokran and her father's other children were left in the custody of his third wife. Her stepmother was a lawyer, and she often pulled all-nighters at the office. Not long after this latest marriage, one of the stepbrothers, the first wife's oldest son, molested Mokran while she was asleep. After her father found out and nearly beat the boy to death, the son ran out of the house and stole a car parked in front of a restaurant. Around four in the morning he crashed into seven parallel-parked cars and was arrested by the police. He had been driving drunk without a license, and the taxi driver pursuing him was injured and hospitalized.

"In English my name's Mulan. That's what it says on my passport too. Did you see the movie?"

Jae nodded. He had watched Disney's film about the girl in ancient China who, disguised as a man, went to war in her father's place.

"To quote my father, mine's the perfect name for the global age, and for the approaching reunification of North and South, something like that. Easy to pronounce in English, comprehensible in Chinese, a name the North Koreans would like . . . All bullshit, like a leopard changing its spots. His daughter's out begging for food on the streets and he's going on about the global age? 'Joseon Homeless Kid Yeom Mokran.' Doesn't it have a nice ring?"

She laughed, then said, "You're kind of different."

"Me? I'm pretty ordinary. You seem more different than me."

"No, you're the different one. You've got a way of seeing inside people. It's like I've been found out."

He shook his head. "No, I can't get inside you."

"You're hilarious. What are you talking about? Get inside me? You an X-Man or something? An alien?"

"It's like when I saw a tiger at the zoo. We were able to look deep into each other's eyes, and for a short while, we understood each other. But when the tiger turned around and disappeared, it was as if it had never happened. I don't know what you're like yet, but for a minute there, I felt we understood each other."

"I've never seen a real tiger. But you're saying it's a good thing, right? That somehow, we get each other."

"Yeah. Me and people, we, well, how can I explain? I mean, it's usually hard for me to connect."

Just when Mokran was about to ask him what he did connect with, some b-boys showed up behind Jae. The concert hadn't been over for long, and the dancer still gave off an overheated energy. They dragged him into the dark alley behind the cultural center.

"You ran away from home?" asked a short, stocky b-boy.

Jae said it was something like that. The same guy, maybe their leader, moved in closer. Jae thought fists might start flying, and tightened his stomach. The guy spoke to him in a low voice. Maybe it was the guy's hip-hop-style clothes that gave Jae the impression, but even the way he spoke sounded like rap.

"A lot of kids who come here have run away from home. Yeah, like you. I don't know why they show up here, but they do.

I guess they feel comfortable here. There's lots of kids like them. Maybe our group members have run away too, yeah, I guess you could see it that way. I mean, we're here day and night, killing time. Still, we haven't really run away. We come since we don't have anywhere else to practice. You know how much we practice a day? We crash in the same room, eat instant noodles, soaked in the smell of our sweat and stinking feet, all day long, yeah, sometimes we're at it practicing over twelve hours a day. At school they call us problem kids. So we don't go to school. Sure, a few of us've left home too. But we've got a place for all of us to sleep, we've got work to do. That's how we're different from you guys. You jerks run away and hang around without a plan, we don't like you. If kids like you keep hanging around, the brass will come. They don't see straight so, shit, they can't tell the difference between you guys and us. They keep putting the screws on us for no reason at all. Fuck, they first say that we're young and tell us to name our school. But we're long past that. Some of us dropped out, others got kicked out. Anyway, that's the way it is. Then the brass says they're going to call our parents. Our parents know we're b-boying, but even if they've given up on us, who wants to be called by the cops in the middle of the night? Why the hell do our parents have to show up late at night at the police station? We didn't do anything criminal, and we didn't run away or anything. But that's nothing. Say you end up on *PD Notebook* or some news show like that. The board of education, city hall, the district office, the cops all show up and destroy this place. You guys can hang around for a few days, then bounce, but not us. This is our bread and butter. You get me?"

"You're asking me to leave, correct?" said Jae.

"Right, that's it. I didn't say you should go home. You can beg, be a delivery boy, it's your life. But don't hang around here. This time we're telling you nicely. Next time we won't."

Jae had just seen how strong they were. He was impressed by their one-handed handstands — bodies frozen in midair, supporting their weight without a tremor — and the drill position, spinning with such force that their heads seemed to dig into the ground. It was impossible to stand up to them. They looked about three or four years older, and Jae lacked their strength, brawn, and speed. And they were only trying to protect their turf. But one thing didn't sit well with him. Why didn't they push back against those stronger than them (the police, parents, and school authorities), instead of pushing around weaker, defenseless kids who had no one?

"I heard that hip-hop isn't about being forceful with the weak and weak with the strong," Jae said. "It isn't just about spinning longer, jumping higher, or doing more powerful moves."

Another b-boy stepped forward. He was a head taller than Jae. "If you're going to say shit you picked up on the Internet about the spirit of hip-hop, forget it. It looks like you haven't been on the streets long, so let me teach you something. If you're just stopping by, it'll seem like everything's chill. There's a stage and there are b-boys. A DJ, an MC, even an amplifier. Cool, everything looks peaceful and orderly, right? And there are girls cheering. But if you think this is the real story, you're a fucking fool. Out here, shit, it's a jungle. America? America's great. Hip-hop? You heard how the oppressed blacks resist by spraying the hell out of alleyways with graffiti, and then meet to battle one on one, right? You can't mess around with the blacks in America. There's a lot of them and they've got political power. Us? Shit, teenage dropouts aren't even human beings. If there's a class is-sue in the Republic of Korea, we're at the bottom. If they step on us, we're stepped on. Resistance? Sure, resist all you want, you shit-talking asshole."

He held up his right hand to Jae's face. His index finger was shorter than the others. "I got my draft notice, so I closed my eyes and cut it right off."

When Jae left Daehangno and headed down toward Dongdae-mun Market, Mokran followed him.

"Those older guys, they're like that to everybody." Mokran tried to comfort him. "They're good enough to enter interna-tional competitions, but if they so much as breathe wrong, the police or the media's all over them."

"I guess they leave girls alone," Jae said calmly.

Mokran changed the subject. "You have somewhere to go?"

"Let's say I was born where two streets meet. I'll keep living on the streets, I've got a feeling."

"Why're you talking like a middle-aged man? 'I was born where two streets meet'?"

"I sound like a real clown, don't I?"

"A little." Mokran giggled. "Do you have a cell phone?"

"Cell phone?" Jae said. "No."

She took his palm and wrote her number on it.

Jae studied his palm and cocked his head. "Aren't you miss-ing a digit?"

"The last digit's three. Memorize it."

From then on, Mokran equaled three to him. Even when he had forgotten her looks and her voice, the number three made him think of her and made an impact on him.

Jae said, "Can I use your cell phone for a minute?"

Mokran handed it over, and Jae began dialing.

14

I WAS ON MY WAY HOME FROM CRAM SCHOOL WHEN
I saw Jae's call.

Jae told me that he had run away from the orphanage and was in Seoul. I asked him where he was calling from.

"Daehangno."

"That's close to me," I said. "Do you have somewhere to sleep?"

He said he had found a bathroom that kept the heating on at night. "I'll need to be out before the older homeless men come in the morning to wash their hair."

I told him to come to my house.

"It's okay. Wandering suits me better." He seemed worried that he'd be sent back to the facility. "I'll call again later."

"Are you calling on someone's phone?"

"Yeah. Someone I met in Daehangno. But I've got to go now." Jae hung up and returned the phone to Mokran.

"What did I say the last digit to my number was?" she asked.

"Three."

"Good. Now you can go."

Mokran saw Jae off. A drunk shouted as he crossed the park. Jae headed toward the city center, where he wouldn't rile the b-boys. He needed to find a place to sleep. Though it was early April, the weather was still too chilly to sleep outdoors. He finally found an alley in the Central Market in eastern Seoul and squeezed himself into a small space between a restaurant supply store and a tableware store, where he stayed alert nearly all night. From somewhere he heard dogs, trapped and whimpering in a cage, waiting to be sold for meat. Like a muscle throbbing after a rigorous workout, his mind didn't calm easily.

Jae learned from the b-boys that he was surrounded by the gaze of hunters, and that those hunters weren't grownups but guys his age. Other similar experiences followed. If he so much as showed up, the others noticed him right away. No matter how quickly he tried to pass through, they recognized him. These groups had a frightening ability to spot solitary homeless boys and always banished them from their turf.

Drifting like this, Jae learned to collect coins from the slots in vending machines. He decided on a district, and all day long, he visited its machines. He stayed nimble and vigilant in order to stay under the radar of the maintenance people and other guys. He grew familiar with the traffic light intervals at intersections and the flow of traffic on the side streets. When he dug out coins, he used his left hand, as it was a bit smaller. He managed to earn around two to three thousand *won* a day this way, enough to buy a rice-and-vegetable roll at the market.

15

JAE USED THE LAST OF HIS MONEY AT A CYBERCAFÉ.
It had been three weeks since he had been out on the streets,
and the weather was terrible that day. He didn't think he could
bear another sleepless night in the spring rain, and older homeless people usually filled up the underground passages. He sat
beside three guys his age who were huddled around a multi-
player game.

"Hey, you!" A guy wearing a grubby white hoodie called Jae
over. He was the biggest of the lot. There was black fuzz above
his lip that made him look even more grown-up.

"What do you want?"

"You ran away from home?"

"Something like that. Why?"

"You alone?"

"No, I'm meeting someone."

"Bullshit, I know you're alone!"

"Okay, fine. I'm alone."

"Hey, this bastard says he's alone," said Hoodie to the boys
beside him. He tapped Jae on the shoulder. "Wanna join us?"

He recognized the game they were playing, a strategy simu-
lation game that he had once played in elementary school. He
said, "I'm no good at it."

"We just need you to make the teams equal."

One of their team members hadn't shown up; Jae ended up

on Hoodie's side against the other two. The game turned out to be fun. Hoodie was an excellent player and made up for Jae's weaknesses, and though they ultimately lost, it wasn't by much. During the game, Jae got a feel for who they were. As soon as the game ended, Hoodie stood up, grabbed his bag, and said to the other two, "Hey, let's get the fuck out of here."

Jae stood up. "Where you going?"

A guy wearing a New York Yankees cap told him off. "Why the hell do you want to know?"

Jae gathered his courage and warily explained that he was broke and had to leave the Internet café. If they had somewhere to sleep, could they put him up for a night?

Baseball Cap grinned. "We let the idiot into one game, and now he thinks he can hang with us."

Hoodie approached Jae. "Will you be our slave?"

"Slave?"

"Don't know what a slave is? It's doing whatever you're told."

The three waited for his response. He didn't feel like he had much of a choice. "Okay. I'll do it."

Baseball Cap interrupted, trying to stop Hoodie. "Shit. What're you doing, bringing a bastard we just met with us? Let's go. Fuck, let's just leave."

"Where are you going?" Jae asked again.

"Give it up." A kid with a pierced ear threatened Jae. "You don't need to know, asshole. Just keep your head down and play your game. Fucking dirty bastard."

Hoodie said, "The bastard says he'll be a slave. Does Your Highness want to be our slave instead?"

Piercing backed off and spit on the floor.

Hoodie turned to Jae. "Look, we're going to meet some girls

first. There's supposed to be four of them, but we're only three, so if there's us three and you, it'll be just right."

"Hey, asshole, I said leave him out. He smells, for real. I'm serious." Baseball Cap frowned.

Hoodie suddenly became angry. "Jesus, you're fucking freaking out. Did you bring us all together? You're a moocher yourself, and you can't seem to shut up. Shut your trap, you cunt."

Baseball Cap continued grumbling, but he backed down. Hoodie grabbed Jae's arm and pulled him up from the chair.

Jae said, "You know, I already paid the nightly rate for the games here . . ."

Jae was holding back, so Hoodie pulled Jae even harder. He said, "Fuck the flat rate. Might as well be the rate of cum coming out of your dick."

The other two laughed as if he'd just told a great joke. Jae gave up and followed them out.

Hoodie gave him a basic orientation that sounded like code. "Hey, you're last. We pick first, then you. If you get stuck with a fuckin' mess, don't grumble. If there's only three vaginas, you'll have to do your own hand job. Got it? Don't get all resentful. And keep your mouth shut. Don't even open that mouth of yours tonight."

They met the girls in front of a shopping mall in the Dong-daemun district. As if they had been built on an assembly line, the girls were the same height and dressed alike in skinny jeans, tight T-shirts, and cheap cardigans. They had caked on their makeup, which may have made them look three or four years older than the guys. But their attitude and expressions gave away their youth. One of the girls stood out. She had bright eyes and a heart-shaped face, and the boys kept looking her way. A girl with hair like sesame leaves negotiated on their behalf, and a girl with two rhinestone barrettes stood behind her, as if assisting her, blowing bubbles with her gum.

"Should we eat something first?" Hoodie asked.

Everyone agreed. They made their way to a cheap joint nearby and sat down. The girls ate enormous quantities of spicy rice cakes and blood sausage. They ate as if they hadn't eaten all day.

"So, why'd you take so long to come out?" Hoodie asked.

"It was tough coordinating our schedules," Sesame Leaf Hair answered.

The girls laughed. The three girls had waited for the last one, the pretty one, to run away together. If they didn't have a pretty girl with them, their attempt at running away would only end in failure. On their first night away, or — at the very latest — by their second, they had to find a roof to sleep under, and to find a guy who would give them a place to sleep. A pretty girl was mandatory. Past experience had taught them that only one of them needed to be pretty for them to be successful on the market for runaways, so they coaxed and scared the cute one, who had been wavering, and finally won her over.

The cute girl's name was Jiyeon, and though her face wasn't symmetrical, something about her kept you looking. The boys bought *soju* and snacks and headed for the semi-basement of a multi-unit where Hoodie lived alone. His parents used to live there, but had moved into his grandfather's house after he passed away. He and his sister lived in the two-bedroom basement, but she hadn't been around for over two months.

"She's like that," Hoodie spat out.

The boys descended into the house in one swoop, but the girls stayed behind and argued with one another. Only when Hoodie came back for them did the girls descend one by one into the semi-basement. They got drunk and started playing a stripping game. Each time they lost, they had to take off a piece of clothing. One of the girls finally had to take off her jeans, leaving only her bra and panties on. "Woah, woah, woah!" shouted the boys. Their voices were changing with puberty, so they sounded like wailing orangutans.

The game continued.

All their eyes were on Jiyeon, who continued losing her clothes. Jae too was down to his underwear. The stink and heat of eight bodies flooded the basement room. Except for Jae, it seemed as if everyone had played the game more than a few times. They screamed and cackled, but gave in to the rules. They knew how things would end. But did they really know? Jae was afraid. His eyes briefly met Jiyeon's, then slid away.

One by one, the girls exposed their breasts. Jae was a little shocked to see that the girls so similar in height and fashion had such different breasts. One girl's were already rounded out like a grownup's, another had breasts that hadn't filled out with fat yet. One had long and perky yellow melons, and another round and firm peaches. They were drunk and excited, and their breathing became ragged as the game sped up. Finally when one girl (probably Rhinestone) stripped off her last article of clothing — her underwear — the game ended because Sesame Leaf Hair stood up and started screaming, "Shit, are we just going to keep playing games forever?"

Hoodie (he'd taken the hoodie off, but Jae didn't know what

else to call him) stood up and slapped Sesame Leaf Hair's cheek. "Bitch!" he said. Everyone laughed noisily, even the girl who'd been hit.

"Why'd you do that, it hurts," she whined, still laughing. He grabbed her arm and took her into the bedroom, skipping over the bags of chips scattered across the floor. Baseball Cap took that as a signal and grabbed Jiyeon, whom he'd been eyeing all along, by the wrist. The problem began there, when she turned him down. He turned to Rhinestone and Bubble Gum in disbelief. The girls tried to calm him down and took Jiyeon into a corner. Though they were whispering, everyone could hear them.

They asked her, "You don't want to put out, or you don't like him?"

She frowned. "I don't want any of it."

"Do you know what it's like to go hungry? We've come all the way here and you say you don't want to? You want to sleep out on the street?"

"I don't know. I just don't want to. I don't feel too good today, either."

The bed was creaking noisily from the bedroom. Baseball Cap, who was pacing nervously, couldn't wait any longer and grabbed Jiyeon.

"Bitch, you playing with me?"

Jae jumped up and gripped Baseball Cap by the waist, and knocked him over. Baseball Cap shook Jae's arm off and kneed him in the face until Jae fell over, his nose bleeding. Baseball Cap used all his strength to kick him repeatedly in the stomach.

One of the girls laughed and said, "Wow, it's a soccer kick."

Baseball Cap burst into the bedroom and in the middle of

the struggling bodies, shouted at Hoodie, "Hey, come out here. Quick!"

Hoodie came out, his hair a mess. When the girls in the corner saw Hoodie's penis hanging out, they backed away. Hoodie, who understood the situation immediately, screamed, "Bitches! If you don't want to do it, fuck off! I was going to let you sleep here, but you're fucking acting up! Fuck!"

Shocked, the girls gave up cajoling Jiyeon and instead snatched her by the hair and pulled her to the floor. Wearing only her underwear, Jiyeon lay sprawled flat like a crushed can of Coke. Sesame Leaf Hair, who rushed out from the bedroom naked, kicked Jiyeon in the face. Rhinestone lit up and dragged on a cigarette, and approached her. Everyone except Jae knew what she was going to do with the cigarette. Only when Jae saw the way Jiyeon looked at the burning tip of the cigarette did he understand. Rhinestone thrust the cigarette end against Jiyeon's thigh. Jiyeon cried and said she was sorry, then Rhinestone and Bubble Gum pulled her up by her armpits and dragged her into the other bedroom. Baseball Cap stripped off his underwear and ran in, and this time, Hoodie followed. Piercing, who had just come out of the bathroom, joined them. They heard the three guys noisily attacking Jiyeon. Like handball athletes after the first half of a match, the other girls had collapsed on the floor and were smoking. Their breasts and legs were completely exposed, and their legs, thighs, and arms were covered with cigarette burns and self-inflicted scars. They looked vacant, as if they had just woken from a deep sleep.

Only Sesame Leaf Hair went to the next room and screeched, "Hey, don't be too rough with her. You'll mess her up." That was it.

Jae quickly got up and went to the bathroom. He threw up everything he had eaten into the dirty toilet. Maybe it was the spicy rice cakes, but his vomit exploded out with a red tint. He was dizzy, but unsure whether it was the alcohol or the events unfolding in front of him. As soon as he left the bathroom, he collapsed in the corner. As he slowly slipped into a foggy sleep, the kids continued to swap partners and have sex.

Jae finally came to the next afternoon. The kids were hanging out and eating deep-fried snacks. The girls took turns showering and fixing their makeup, and some guys played a shooting game on the computer and others played rock, paper, scissors with the girls. What confused Jae most was that no trace remained of what had happened the night before. Jiyeon, who had taken multiple sex partners under threat of more cigarette burns, was joking around with the guys and chatting with the girls. Overnight, order had been restored. Jae understood. This wasn't the world of human beings; it was the world of animals.

The guys tapped Jae's head.

One laughed. "Fool, heard you fainted."

"Watch, a bastard like this goes at it later even fucking harder," another added.

Baseball Cap frowned fiercely and threatened Jae. "You do that one more time and I'll fucking kill you. What's our goddamn slave doing, getting all cocky?"

Jae merely ate the cold fried snacks. From his corner, he watched the kids. The unofficial leaders of the group, Hoodie and Sesame Leaf Hair, began organizing the house like a married couple. They consulted each other on all important matters, and everyone else respected their decisions. It was clear that if they didn't, they would be punished. You could say it was a nightmarish version, or a pornographic one, of the way they had once played house on the playground. The eight boys and girls moved back and forth in the narrow house like ants. Only Jae bothered to clean the bathroom; it was even dirtier than the public ones at the bus terminal. There were no cleaning products around, so he made foam out of body soap and used that. He had sometimes done this kind of work at the orphanage. When Piercing had to pee and discovered Jae cleaning, he opened the door wide for all to see. Everyone laughed for no reason. Piercing made a big show of peeing into the just scrubbed toilet bowl, noisily spraying everywhere.

The girls were sitting at the computer, logged onto Cyworld. They had nothing in the real world, but all kept up fancy profile rooms in cyberspace. They were trashing a girl they knew online, endlessly swapping insults about her. If they ever went back to school, the first thing they would do was take care of that bitch. They moved on to another site and were diligently tapping away at the keyboard when Sesame Leaf Hair went outside and answered a call. She returned, pumping her fist in the air, and screamed, "Yes!"

They were all thrilled, looking into the mirror, fixing their makeup, and rushing around.

One said to the boys, "We'll be back."

"You better come back with some fried chicken. The spicy kind."

"Got it."

After the girls disappeared, the house felt deserted.

"Where are they going?" Jae asked.

Hoodie snickered. "To get fried chicken."

A few hours later, the girls actually did return with fried

chicken. Only Bubble Gum looked a little blue; the others were full of their usual cheer. Bubble Gum went into the bathroom and didn't come out for a long time. It was clear she was crying. The other girls ate the fried chicken and rattled on about the pervert that Bubble Gum had ended up with, as if to show off their battle stories.

All the days bled into each other. Day and night, the girls left to earn money and returned with fried chicken, pizza, soft drinks, and *soju*. Jae tidied up after the boys and girls. He emptied ashtrays, cleaned vomit, and went on errands to buy sanitary pads and cigarettes. Still every night, the house returned to chaos. The stripping game was no longer needed; the kids had wild sex without condoms or birth control pills. Hoodie told Sesame Leaf Hair to help Jae lose his virginity, as if doing him a favor, but she immediately refused. She said that Jae was "dirty and gross," but she seemed more wary of Baseball Cap. The other girls were in the same boat.

One day at dawn, Jae discovered Jiyeon curled up asleep beside him. He tentatively stroked the fair, smooth skin of her face, then slid his tongue in between her lips. She didn't know who it was, but she accepted it out of habit. She slowly woke up. When her bleary eyes opened and she saw whose tongue had entered her mouth, she bolted up and screamed as if the experience was new to her and it was the most horrific thing in the world.

The girls woke up, and eventually Baseball Cap and Piercing came out to the living room and started thrashing Jae. They didn't even ask what had happened — they just automatically began stomping on him. Only Jiyeon stopped him from being beaten to death.

"He didn't have me," she said. "Don't hit him, let up."

But the beating stopped only when Hoodie intervened. "You wanna go to reform school? Quit it."

Baseball Cap dragged a tearful Jiyeon into the bedroom. He laid her on the floor and spread her legs open, and got on top of her. Jae crawled to the bathroom and washed his face. His entire body was burning. He couldn't tell if it was from raging, murderous thoughts or from lust. He was at the age when it was hard to tell the difference. If something was boiling, the boiling was all he could feel. When Jae left the bathroom, his eyes fixed on a fruit knife left after someone had sliced up an apple. Rhinestone, who must have sensed a menacing energy in him, silently took his arm. This hand that had nearly scarred her friend's face with a cigarette was surprisingly warm, tender. Only when she embraced him did he realize that she was naked. Those days it was as if they were naked when dressed, and dressed when naked. Only when she kneeled and sucked on his penis did he forget the knife. He began crying, then ejaculated in her mouth. She gazed up into his face, but he avoided her and left quietly.

The alley was peaceful. No one seemed to know that right in front of them, young fourteen-year-old girls were hustling on the streets and having group sex at night. A woman in her fifties throwing out garbage glanced furtively at Jae, then hurriedly returned to her house. No, he thought. Maybe everyone actually does know. They're just ignoring it. On top of the red brick wall, a tabby cat in heat screeched. Jae asked himself, Why on earth do things like this happen? There was no answer. His entire body began trembling. Finally, he returned to their world.

Soon small changes began to happen. Group sex became less frequent (though it didn't disappear) and couples paired up. Bubble Gum began having diarrhea, so she returned home, reducing the number of girls to three. Hoodie slept with Sesame Leaf Hair and Jiyeon slept with Baseball Cap. Piercing, with Rhinestone. Jae continued as a slave. Sometimes when the girls were drunk, they helped relieve his sexual needs using one method or another, almost out of kindness.

As time passed, the girls began to have more influence. Whether it was because they were the ones bringing in the money, or if that was how it always went, Jae wasn't sure. The guys began to listen to Sesame Leaf Hair's nagging. The house became a little cleaner, which the boys didn't mind. When the girls brought home money, they all went to a cybercafé and played an Internet game or went to karaoke and jumped around singing. Sometimes they put Jiyeon on video chat to lure men in, then sent out Rhinestone or Sesame Leaf Hair instead. While one girl stayed inside the motel, the other girls paced back and forth outside, holding their phones. While this was happening, the boys lazed around at home and played computer games.

"Leave her alone today. She isn't in good shape," Sesame Leaf Hair said to the boys.

That day Rhinestone had been forced to have group anal sex with two men. The girls lifted Rhinestone up from the floor in their arms and cried together. After wailing for some time, they fixed their makeup, said they were going to cheer themselves up, and went to karaoke. The girls came back with busted-up hands. When asked what happened, they said they had run into an old enemy at the worst time and place and punched her right in her trap. On Baseball Cap's birthday, the girls returned with a cake. They opened a bottle of cheap champagne and lit some firecrackers, and smeared the cake all over Baseball Cap's face. The boys stripped him down and said it was a birthday beating before they stepped all over him. Even though they broke one of his front teeth, he grinned happily. Later he got drunk and imitated a comedian playing the village fool, saying, "Baseball Cap is nowhere!" They laid him down on his stomach and pounded him on the back, singing, *"Why were you born, you asshole? Why were you ever born, you asshole? Why were you born into this fucked-up world?"*

"Are you going to keep living like this?" Jae cautiously asked Hoodie one night. The girls were out and the boys were sitting around watching TV. At first Hoodie didn't seem to understand what he'd asked. Hoodie's mouth hung open and he looked perplexed, as if Jae had spoken in a foreign language.

"This? What do you mean by 'this'?" He seemed annoyed and continued chewing on cold leftover chicken.

Jae scanned the room. "This, like here now. With the girls."

"What about 'with the girls'? You mean how long is this craziness going to last? Why? You don't like it? Then fuck off."

"I didn't mean it like that, I was just curious. So it's always going to be like this?"

Jae readied himself in case Hoodie suddenly attacked him, but Hoodie shrugged. "The bitches'll leave soon enough."

"Where'll they go? When?"

"Who knows. Fuck, we just take what they've got until we can't. The bitches don't last long."

"What do you mean, don't last long? You mean they go back home?"

"Well, there probably isn't a single one who wants to go back. But they don't have anywhere else to go, do they? They just go on like this until they start having problems with each other. They gang up on one of the girls, or they take sides and fight, then suddenly, *pow!*"

Hoodie laughed. "They fight like hell, then when they leave, they leave together. Go figure."

"Why do they fight?"

Hoodie stared blankly at Jae, then grinned. "Why do they fight?"

He took a swift look around the room, then spat out, "Is this any way for a person to live?"

It didn't sound like something a teenager would say.

"It's the fucking thing you do at one point in your life. Hell, how could we do this all the time? Maybe these retarded girls have low IQs, or maybe they're worn-out hos to start with, 'cause they forget quickly. They crawl back home at the end, then when they find another group member, they crawl out again. Eventually they all crawl back again."

"So that's how it is."

"Why? Is there a girl you wanna see again?"

"No."

"Bullshit. You're always looking at Jiyeon."

Jae stayed silent.

"Why? 'Cause of the fucker Jongwook?" That was Baseball Cap's name. "Move over him, you idiot."

"Aren't you two friends?"

"Friends? That asshole and me?" Hoodie laughed. "Friends, what a load of shit. Stop talking shit and let's shoot some guns."

The two sat in front of a computer, shooting and killing thousands of terrorists. Giants with bombs strapped to them, carrying grenade launchers and AK-47s, collapsed as their bodies sprayed blood and bone marrow. The bottom of the screen turned blood red.

The girls came back. Baseball Cap woke up from a long nap, smelling pizza. Jae took a beer out of the cabinet and, while Baseball Cap was stuffing pizza into his mouth, struck him from behind with the bottle. Baseball Cap — caught entirely off guard — collapsed without a word. The girls shrieked as Jae kicked Baseball Cap in the stomach. No one knew why and no one dared ask. After Piercing grabbed Jae by the waist, the girls dragged Baseball Cap into the next room. Hoodie sat and quietly continued eating, and Jiyeon, terrified, stayed close to the sink and watched.

Even after Baseball Cap came to, he crept around Jae, before stealthily sneaking out of the house. Only Hoodie spoke to him with a halfhearted "See you later." The rest ignored him. When night came, Jae took Jiyeon by the wrist and pulled her under his blanket. No one stopped him.

"Just don't come inside me," Jiyeon asked, frowning as soon as he entered her.

Jae wasn't sure what this meant, so he wasn't able to do what she asked. His first sexual experience ended abruptly. Jiyeon stepped over Jae, who had collapsed feeling as if he'd been beaten in the head, and ran to the bathroom. He listened to the successive *stomp, stomp, stomp* of her feet.

She said, "If you do this, you're less likely to get pregnant. But next time, can you pull out?"

He promised. The next morning while Jae was wiping up bloodstains from the floor — remains of his assault on Baseball

Cap — Hoodie passed him and said, "Clean it with cold water. That's how you get blood out."

That afternoon Jae went out to the store for instant noodles and bleach. On his return, he saw an unfamiliar van in front of the house that hadn't been there before. He saw five burly men inside, watching the entrance of Hoodie's semi-basement. Jae positioned himself farther away and continued watching. The car door opened, the men checked their surroundings, then headed toward the house. One man rang the bell and the others lingered, waiting. But as soon as the door opened, they forced themselves in. The five kids were dragged out, one after another. Jiyeon hadn't had time to put sneakers on — she was wearing only a single Adidas slipper. Jiyeon, Sesame Leaf Hair, and Rhinestone were hauled away in an old sedan parked thirty or so meters away. A stakeout car. Baseball Cap had clearly blown the whistle.

The neighbors were watching this commotion happening in broad daylight and clicking their tongues, looking as if such a sight stretched far beyond their imagination.

16

JAE CONTINUED TO ENDURE MORE OF THE SAME.

Dirty, small houses, *soju* bottles and chicken bones scattered across rooms, boys and girls drinking nightly and acting violent over nothing at all. I don't want to write any more about it, but I should cover the last and most horrifying group of kids that Jae faced before I move on. They were led by a seventeen-year-old guy who essentially imprisoned a mentally impaired girl named Hanna and lived off her basic living assistance and disability allowance. They met Hanna in an online chatroom. After the guy first managed to enter her house, he called his younger sister, Geumhui, and his friend from middle school, Nike.

Jae met Geumhui while eating instant noodles at a convenience store, and she immediately took to him. "You're kinda cute," she said. "I've got a place to sleep — you want to come with me?"

He had no reason not to, so he followed her. On the way there, they found a mattress that someone had thrown out. Geumhui asked Jae to help her bring it back, but he said he could carry it on his own and quickly lifted it up. It was something he had done at the orphanage on big cleaning days.

"All you have to do is center it just right," he said.

The two guys would beat Hanna at any little excuse. When they did, Geumhui would avoid them by surfing the web or staying near Jae. One very stupid reason they hit Hanna was because she officially "belonged" to the leader, but the leader caught her kissing Nike one day. Actually Nike was molesting Hanna when the leader caught them. Leader pulled Nike aside and asked him for the full story. Nike made excuses, saying that Hanna had made a pass at him. When the boys calmed down, Leader and Nike tied Hanna to a chair and began punishing her. They repeatedly asked her, "Why'd you make a pass at Nike?"

It was torture for the sake of torture, but once they started, they couldn't stop — Leader didn't want to look weak in front of Nike, Nike was afraid that Leader would misunderstand him, and Geumhui didn't want to appear to be on Hanna's side. Hanna, who had a low IQ and was slow to understand what others wanted, offered irrelevant answers, and each time, the two guys increased the intensity of the torture. They heated a spoon over the gas range and pressed it against her thigh. They tied her to the chair and made her sleep there. When she wet herself, they said she was filthy and beat her for that too.

Jae asked Geumhui how she could let this happen. Shouldn't she tell her brother to stop? Geumhui kept her eyes on the computer game she was playing and said coldly, "It's none of your business. She's got to be punished."

Days later, the guys went to the bank to collect Hanna's monthly check and Geumhui went to the hair salon. Hanna was still tied to the chair. Alone with her, Jae felt his soul palpitating about the room for the first time in ages. He relived the confusion of his solitary confinement at the orphanage, when his consciousness freed itself from his body and sought another host. The cheaply made plywood chair from China was in agony, and the impact shook Jae. The chair had lost its composure, its rage had increased beyond the critical limit, and its cracked voice released a mangled grammar of rapid-fire sentences. It was suffering and humiliated by Hanna's leaking body fluids. The chair had absorbed her pain, which went against the nature of the chair, whose pride lay in its usefulness. Jae untied Hanna's restraints.

"Go and tell your daddy everything, about how the kids are bullying you."

Her alcoholic father worked as a day laborer at construction sites. Occasionally he stopped by before work to see Hanna, but he only seemed relieved that the kids were helping out his handicapped daughter.

Jae added, "You better run away fast before the others come. Quick!"

Hanna shook her head and said that she was in love with Leader.

"Do you even know what love means?"

"I'm not stupid. I know what love is. I love him. Because he loves me, he's doing this. I can bear it. Tie me up again," she entreated, lisping as she held two hands out.

"You're asking me to tie you up again?"

"Yes."

"I can't do that."

"I want it. I want it. I said I want it!"

She kept stubbornly whining, then she cried. She began to hit Jae. She stank of urine.

"Then at least take a shower," he said.

She shook her head adamantly. "I hate showers."

She blamed her suffering on kissing Nike, and now Jae was asking her to erase all the evidence of her reparation. She simply wanted to return to the way she was before Leader came back.

Jae was fed up with her blind refusal to understand, so he tied her up again. Each time the chair squeaked loudly, it sounded like a scream.

"I won't tell," Hanna said. "I won't tell anyone," as if she were doing him a favor. Leader was about a head taller than Jae; he wouldn't be able to defeat Leader in a fight. On top of that, he was always with Nike. But even if he were able to fight them and win, wasn't it pointless? If you lowered a rope to a soul fallen into a pit, and the soul didn't have the will to take the rope and climb, all that effort was wasted. Whether he slashed tires or toppled formidable enemies, nothing changed. *Is this just because I'm young?* he wondered. *Because I have no power and don't know enough about the world?* Jae, who had never been religious, found himself thinking of God. It seemed impossible for anyone except God to find a way out of this situation. He thought of reporting it to the police. But if Hanna denied it, the boys would be released immediately and return to her.

As soon as Geumhui got back from the hairdresser, Jae said, "You should untie Hanna."

"Me? Why?"

"You have to untie her. Come on, do it fast."

"I can't. My brother won't put up with it."

"If you don't untie her, I'm going to leave."

She looked closely at Jae to see if he meant it. He said more firmly, "Untie her. Tell your brother later."

"I can't do that. I mean, she did make a move on him."

"Stop talking crap. Is it because you think it'll be easier for you with her like this? That it?"

Geumhui scrutinized him. "The little bitch! Did she try making a move on you too? Huh?"

She took Hanna by the hair and began shaking her. Hanna collapsed and Jae grabbed Geumhui by the neck. She squirmed and struggled, but as soon as Jae punched her in the stomach, she doubled over. Hanna, who hadn't cried when she was beaten, wailed like an injured heifer. Jae released Hanna and pulled Geumhui up, seating her on Hanna's chair. Then he bound her.

Geumhui implored, "I love you. You know I love you, don't you? Why're you doing this? Seriously. Why?"

But Jae didn't listen. He left Hanna in the other room and waited for the others to return. He also hid a knife in the pot of the shriveled-up rubber tree, just in case.

At first Leader and Nike didn't catch on. They tossed off their shoes and entered. When they heard the screaming and sobbing, they halted. But they didn't understand. How could the girl tied to the chair be Geumhui and not Hanna? Jae pulled the bathroom door open, walked out, and faced the boys, with the chair between them.

Leader's forearms slowly flexed. His voice shook as he said, "Fuck, what kind of crazy shit is this?"

"Huh? What crazy shit?" Jae asked calmly.

Geumhui screamed, "That crazy bastard, he's out of his mind. Untie me quick. My arms hurt so much, I think I'm gonna die."

Nike said, "This shit tied you up?"

"He even punched me in the stomach. I thought I was gonna die. That bastard, he's gone crazy, the asshole."

"So why'd you bring the fucker here?"

"I said untie me, quick."

Leader didn't take his eyes off Jae. He seemed to think that

Jae might attack while he was untying his sister. Nike swerved around the chair and slowly moved toward Jae.

"You better not get any closer," Jae said.

Leader looked at Nike, who was approaching Jae, telling him to hold back. Then Leader said, "Let me ask you one thing. Why're you doing this? Are you for real crazy?"

"Geumhui made a move on Nike. So I'm punishing her. Why? I can't do that?"

Surprised, Nike screamed, "What kind of bullshit is this?"

Geumhui said, "I told you he's crazy! Why're you still talking to him? Just kill him."

"Okay, let's kill him and bury him," Leader said moodily, and took a cautious step forward.

It dawned on Jae that he might be killed. He thought of the farm engulfed in flames. Of the sound of dogs whimpering all night long, and the peace he felt that night he entered their souls. This erased his fears, and Leader's bluff about burying him actually eased his tension.

"I've got something to ask your little sister. See here, your sister Geumhui made a move on Nike. I need to ask your sister why she did it. You guys stay out of it."

"You asshole, you're unbelievable. Where'd this crazy bastard come from?"

Leader and Nike, unable to take any more, swerved around the chair and sprang at him. As soon as Nike grabbed Jae by the waist of his pants, Leader kicked him near the knee. But Jae didn't give in and punched Leader in the face. As he retreated, he took the knife hidden in the potted plant and brandished it. Like an inline skate when its wheel hits a stone, the knife broke from its arc and made a jagged cut across Nike's shoulder. Blood splattered to the ceiling.

"Aaaack!" Nike screamed as he grabbed his shoulder and collapsed. The knife had cut through the shirt and pierced his shoulder. It felt different, smoother than when he had ripped the tires.

Shocked, Leader stepped back. Nike crawled on his knees through the growing pool of blood, fumbling for a weapon, but Jae had already made sure to remove everything. Leader's pants darkened, absorbing the blood on the floor.

Jae said to Leader, "So you ask your sister. Ask her why she made a move on Nike."

Leader looked wildly around. "If you put the knife down and leave quietly, I won't follow. I promise."

"What? You can't just let that asshole go!" Nike shouted, but Leader continued talking to Jae. Jae heard fear in the subtle quiver of his voice.

"Put the knife down and leave the house. I don't know why you did this, but get out. I have to take him to the hospital — you see, don't you? How much fucking blood he's losing? He'll die without help."

"Get on your knees," Jae demanded.

"What?"

"You heard, didn't you? Get over to the wall."

Surprisingly, without protest Leader went and faced the wall. He sat cross-legged, but he didn't get on his knees.

Jae held the knife to his throat and repeated, "I told you, on your knees."

Only then did Leader listen. Nike crawled on his side and

lay face-down. Geumhui had shut up and was watching Jae in sheer terror.

Jae said, "I'm not trying to be a hero or anything. I'm just saying, shit, no one should ever do what you did to another human being. Is that so hard to understand?"

He pressed the knife to Leader's throat; Leader shook his head.

"It's not hard, is it?" Jae said. "Not hard at all. I'm not hard to understand."

Jae lifted his right foot in the air, like in the movies, and kicked Leader in the back. Leader, still on his knees, fell flat on his face. As Jae left, he glanced over at Geumhui, but she twisted her head to the left and avoided his gaze. Nothing would change. If he came back a few days later, he would find them living in the exact same way. They might be tormenting Hanna even worse than before. But that didn't make Jae feel helpless; he actually felt stronger. His changing self, a growing seed in solitary confinement at the orphanage, was becoming more solid.

As Jae left, he gathered all their shoes and tossed them over the neighboring house's wall. He ran until he hit a safe spot, then stopped to take a deep breath when his chest began throbbing with pain. He saw visions. Baseball Cap on the ground after he had struck him with the bottle. Nike on the ground, bleeding. Jae felt his head splitting and his right shoulder burning as if drenched in scalding water. The pain he had caused Baseball Cap and Nike had ricocheted back to him, and he began to cry. It's unfair, he thought. All of you sinned and all I did was punish you. So why do I have to endure your pain? Even with his eyes closed, the visions continued. He saw Hanna tied to the chair, and Jiyeon burned with a cigarette. Jae's entire body trembled as if he were tied down, unable to move. It was dawn before a security guard in the electronics shopping mall discovered Jae. A scar across his thigh resembled a cigarette burn, and a red laceration across his shoulder, like a knife wound; his arms and legs were nearly paralyzed from lack of circulation, his pants stained with his runny shit and with urine. The guard sprayed water over Jae's face and woke him, then sent him packing.

From then on, Jae kept to himself. He slept in public bathrooms, under building stairwells, and in the basement boiler rooms of apartment complexes with lax security. Everywhere he went was infested with mosquitoes, so his entire body broke out in red spots. He developed dry, flaky patches on his face that resembled a skin disease. A woman who ran one of Seoul's many outdoor drinking tents sometimes gave him free dumplings and spicy rice cakes. When she was in a good mood, she would even hand out a hard-boiled egg. But most days he rummaged through trashcans for his food. Convenience-store rice-and-vegetable rolls past their expiration date were the best, but they weren't easy to find, since the part-time cashiers usually took them. Fast-food chains threw out food with the wrappers intact, and on a good day, he was able to gorge. The first few months he often had diarrhea, but later his stomach adjusted.

A year passed. Jae turned seventeen on the streets. When he hadn't washed for a long time, he resembled a beggar from the countryside. He no longer rummaged through trashcans; instead, he satisfied his dietary needs by eating uncooked rice once a day. He ate the bare minimum and moved quietly. He read books that he found at a recycling collection site, but spent most of his days in quiet spaces, thinking.

PART
THREE

17

THE CAFÉ IN THE BASEMENT OF THE FOUR-STORY
building had a high ceiling, and was open and spacious except
for the hall's four supporting pillars. The black-finished walls
and the alcove radiated a soft yellow light that reminded me a
little of Mama Pig's hostess bar. My gaze naturally strayed to the
center. A bold ray of light beamed from the ceiling, and the air
was smoky from cigarettes and clammy dry ice. The trancelike
electronic music was thick in the air, dividing one person from
another like a curtain. Though the space was crowded with customers, I felt like a solitary alien who had landed on a lonely
planet. This made me think that the rays looked like columns of
light from a UFO, and the people at the tables, earthlings waiting to greet the aliens.

A hexagonal acrylic cube, about two-by-two meters in size,
rested at the base of the columns of light. Inside the cube I saw a
mannequin in skinny jeans and a low-cut white chiffon blouse,
lying at an angle.

I ordered a Coke from the approaching waitress.

Just then, the mannequin began squirming then stood upright. She gazed coolly around her and yawned. The off-white
beam of light moved slowly from her bare feet up to her face.
She was clearly a human being. But because of the lights and
the setting, she looked like a cyborg. I found myself gaping. We
ordinary people emerge into the world as wet, bloody babies

from our mother's womb, but the being inside the cube was far removed from human impurities and our disgusting, frantic lifestyles. It was nearly perfect.

Her work was simple. All she had to do was stay inside the cube and act natural, as if everything outside was a vacuum — a kind of outer space. She had earbuds in and read comic books, surfed the Internet on her netbook, and seemed to chat online with friends. When she was tired, she pulled a Hello Kitty blanket over herself and napped. She drank Welch's juice and ate bites of cheesecake. The entire setup looked like experimental theater, or a popular reality TV show in America, or even a sacrificial offering. It was a space free of anything dirty or messy, a space where you could eat but where excreting was beyond imagination.

I asked the waitress, "Excuse me, but Yeom Mokran — does she work here?"

"If you call what she does work. I don't think she's off yet." The waitress pouted as she pointed at the cube. Though sporadic gusts of dry ice blocked my view, the cube was definitely there.

Once when I was young, my family went to the beach. It was probably somewhere by the East Sea. At night my father took us to a sashimi restaurant. A lone halibut was still alive on the fresh plate that the chef had skillfully prepared for us. I still vividly remember how desperate the halibut looked, with its gaping mouth and bleary eyes. My father said a man needs to know how to eat these kinds of things, and shoved a piece into my mouth.

What I'd felt then came back vividly to me. Mokran's experience in the cube clearly wasn't cruel, but the café owner and the sashimi chef both exposed me to what I didn't care to see — what I'd regret seeing — but was supposed to accept and enjoy.

Mokran had called me the day before. I'd saved her number under Jae's name in my address book, so I assumed it was him, and answered, "Jae, is that you?"

"I'm not Jae," a woman's voice said.

"Then who is this?"

"You're his friend, right?"

"Yes, and?"

"Sounds like you haven't been in touch with him either. You asked right away if it was him."

She wanted to know where Jae was hiding. I wanted to know the same.

"It's weird, I keep wondering about him," she said. "You know, he's the first to get a hold of my number and not call me."

I couldn't think of anything to say so I waited for whatever was next.

She asked, "Which school do you go to?"

When I told her, she said that my school was near where she worked part-time, and that I should drop by when I was free.

"Is it somewhere students can be?" I asked, cautiously using informal language back to her for the first time.

"Yeah, it's just a café," she said. "What, you thought I was some wild chick?"

And now Mokran was locked inside a clear cage, a cube, yawning. I was drinking my Coke with a straw when I recalled the woman trapped in the water tank. The helpless magician and the woman. The air bubbles frothing from her lips. Her swaying body. Thinking about the scene made me feel queasy. I wanted to scream, to run and shatter the cube. It was a stupid thought but I couldn't stop myself.

I shot up from my seat, but dry ice blasted out and the spotlights above dimmed. Like a UFO that had completed its mission, the ray of light aimed at the center of the floor; Mokran became fuzzy, then promptly disappeared. Like an alien temporarily come down to earth: mission completed as time warped.

I went outside but didn't see Mokran, so I leaned against the wall and lit a cigarette. After two smokes I felt calmer, until I heard the rev of an engine. When I turned, I saw a girl on a Kawasaki, wearing goggles but no helmet. I wasn't sure it was Mokran, so I approached cautiously.

"I'm Donggyu, Jae's . . ."

The girl pushed the goggles up to her forehead and squinted at me. "I saw you come into the café. Good to see you."

I was relieved it was Mokran.

"Your motorcycle's . . . cool," I stuttered out as casually as I could.

Mokran looked different in sunlight. Without the lights dramatizing her three-dimensionality in the cube, she didn't feel as mysterious, but she was as pretty as ever.

"It looks like . . . you're going somewhere?"

"Yeah, I've got another part-time job."

As she leaned over the bike saddle, I couldn't take my eyes off her profile.

I asked, "Are you going to be inside something again, like here?"

"No, this time I've got to dance with a bunch of girls for a new store opening. I just have to get on a table and move around."

"Oh."

I saw the hem of her plaid school uniform through the gap

of her backpack. So she would change into the uniform and dance.

Mokran asked, "But Jae — so you really haven't been in touch with him?"

"I've been wondering about him. The last time was on your phone, a year ago, I think."

"I thought you guys were besties. He was a strange kid. If he was hanging around this area, I'd have run into him at least once. If you see him, can you tell him I've been looking for him?"

"He might have caught the devil by now."

Mokran turned back to me. "What are you talking about?"

I told her about how Jae had set two mirrors facing each other in the redevelopment district — and how he had tried to use black magic. She giggled but looked intrigued.

I quickly added, "If he really caught the devil and is ordering him around right now, he might not be in the area."

"You saying that to make me laugh? I get it, you two are a little weird. I'm taking off now."

"Um, if you end up seeing Jae first, tell him to call me."

"Okay," she said.

Mokran roared away on her Kawasaki. From that day onward, I began dreaming about her. In my dreams she's always inside the cube. She's masturbating with a long-haired Jae beside her, looking out of the cube at me. Jae gestures at me to come in, but I can't find the entrance and keep circling. The more he insists, the more stressed I get. Finally Mokran stops touching herself and glares at me. Then she hurls the glass in her hand and screams, "This isn't juice! It's semen!"

18

THE NEXT DAY ON MY WAY BACK FROM LUNCH, A KID
from my class called out to me, "Hey, Farty Donggyu."

That was my nickname at school. My class standing was so
low that I ranked just ahead of a kid so fat he could hardly stand
on his feet. Still I felt like I was dead last. I was no good at studying, no good at fighting. I was a wuss — the ultimate idiot.

"Some weird homeless guy's looking for you," he said.
"Maybe he's your dad."

"Where is he?"

"The stationery store across the street. Get us some pastries
while you're at it."

When I approached the front gate, a guy as skinny as a skewer
was waiting for me.

"Do I know you?" I asked.

"It's me, Jae."

He'd left Seoul for the orphanage two years earlier, at age
fifteen. Though it was more than enough time for a teenager
to change, I was shocked. I barely recognized him. He had shot
up to nearly six feet in height and didn't have an ounce of fat
on him. His cheekbones were burnt red underneath his shaggy
beard, and he had the taut appearance of a knife pinned to a
cutting board.

"Is it really you?"

He was a seventeen-year-old guy who looked like a grownup — which meant he would no longer be let off the hook if caught breaking rules. But his eyes and cheekbones resembled the Jae I knew, and he had the same aura that I remembered from childhood.

He said, "I've changed that much?"

"If we'd accidentally run into each other, I wouldn't have recognized you."

Jae asked me how I was, but I couldn't bring myself to return his question. His appearance was answer enough. We sat on some plastic chairs in front of a convenience store.

"You want something to eat?" I asked.

He shook his head and showed me some uncooked grains of rice that he had pulled out of his pocket.

"What's that?"

"You don't know what rice is?"

Jae tossed a few grains in his mouth and chomped on them. "This is enough for me."

I bought a rice ball from the store and came back out.

"You should have some," I said.

He glanced at it but, as I'd expected, shook his head.

"I saw you in my dream last night," he said.

"That's strange. Yesterday I met a girl named Mokran and we talked about you."

"Mokran? Who's that?"

"She said you'd met a year ago in the Daehangno area. You even called me on her cell, remember?"

Only then did Jae seem to recall her. I told him how we'd met.

"Can I use your phone?" Jae asked. Then after checking, he said, "So it is a three."

"What are you talking about?"

"Her number. Long story."

Jae returned the phone to me and I asked him, "Why don't you call her? Now that it's come to this . . ."

"I wasn't planning on getting in touch with you." He was still chomping on the rice grains.

"Why?"

"You turned me in."

"That's . . ."

"I don't need excuses. I like who I am now."

"Where are you sleeping?"

"There's a lot of places, if you're fine with sleeping in the cold."

"You're sure you don't want some?"

I passed the rice ball to him, but again he shook his head. I finally crammed the rest into my mouth.

"So how've you been?" he asked again.

"My father got remarried. My stepmom has two of her own kids — they're both scared of me and act shocked every time they see me. Their memories seem to reset every morning. It's like they always have a 'Who are you?' look on their faces."

Jae said, "I had a dream yesterday. You were in front of a see-through room. I was inside, but no matter how many times I asked you to come in, you wouldn't. No, actually, it was like you couldn't come in, like you were watching me in a movie."

"Was there a girl there too?"

"No, I only saw you."

"So what happened?"

"Your body exploded. Bang! Like a bomb. It made me hurt all over."

"You felt pain?"

"I'm often in pain these days. It feels like someone's squeezing my heart, like it's a dishtowel."

"Do you think you've got heart problems or something?"

"There's a pattern to it. It doesn't make a difference whether it's an object, machine, animal, or human. If a being experiences extreme suffering, I feel it too."

Jae's sunken eyes became shiny and glowed with an otherworldly energy.

"You just feel pain?"

"Happiness too, if they're happy. But that's less common. It's usually pain."

He recounted all he'd experienced in the past two years. Just listening to his story made me feel terrible, especially the parts about being with the kids who'd run away from home.

"Yesterday I was under one of the Han River bridges, hiding from the rain, when my heart started hurting. I thought of you and I realized you must be in pain."

Jae had once been the interpreter of my desires and now he said he could read my pain. But I didn't want to be such an easy read — like something you could throw away after finishing.

"I'm all right," I said. "Things aren't great with my stepmom, but if I just put up with three more years I'll be off to college."

As soon as I uttered the word "college," guilt overwhelmed me and I looked away.

"Why're you going to college? Do you want to go?"

"I have to go."

"Who said so?"

"The world says so." I felt defensive.

"You really think so?"

"Just because you can't go doesn't make it meaningless. There's a reason why everyone goes."

"All I'm doing is asking questions. This past year I've been asking myself questions over and over. It's habit now, I guess. Why am I suffering? Why does someone else's suffering become my suffering? Why has God given me this fate? What does it mean that even though I was meant to die at the bus terminal, I'm still alive? I wake up early in the morning and wander around all day, reading and thinking. Still, I never have enough time."

"So?" I said. "Did you find your answer?"

"There's something strange growing out of my back. You know, don't you?"

"I know. You used to say it was a vestigial organ, a degenerate wing bone — like our tailbone."

"I was joking, but really, I kind of believed I had a half-formed wing on my back and that someday it would start growing again."

"So has your wing grown out?"

I touched Jae's back. It didn't feel any different from when he had been a kid.

"It's the same," I said.

"I thought I would be like a winged animal from a folktale, but it wasn't like that."

"Then what is it?"

"In our world, there are machines with unique goals called sensors, whose goal is to feel. Sensors all around the world measure the temperature, humidity, and wind speed. Some sensors hang from the branches of fir trees and react and take pictures when a Siberian tiger passes. There are way too many sensors. They read the flaws on a CD, or use infrared light to measure distance between a subject and a lens, but there are no sensors to detect suffering."

"So you're saying that's what you are?"

"That's right," he said. "I think I'm made that way. In the morning when commuters pass by me on the street, their suffering weighs down my soul. My heart feels like it'll explode with the heaviness of their lives."

"Can't you escape it? Don't you want an easier life?"

"It's impossible. This is my fate."

"You've got to come to your senses. You're not a machine, right? God couldn't have just made you feel pain without giving you the power to overcome it."

"This is God's nature. God's an unbalanced sadist. He gives you an unlimited sex drive, but makes it difficult to satisfy. He gives you death, but makes it impossible to avoid. He gives you life, but doesn't tell you why you were born."

"Is there anything I can do to help?"

"No." He laughed and shook his head.

"Really, if there's something I can do, just ask."

Jae silently took another handful of rice grains from his coat pocket and handed it to me. The grains of rice looked whiter on his dirty palm. I took a few grains and shoved them in my mouth. The bell signaling the end of lunch rang. Jae gazed up at the school's clock tower with the eyes of a sailor looking back at the port. As I ran toward class, Jae's last words seized me by the neck.

"You don't need to run," he said. "You're the center of the universe."

Those words made me feel defensive, but I wasn't sure why until later. Something lurked deep inside me and stayed there for a long time.

19

ON A TV IN A SUBWAY STATION, JAE SAW THE B-BOYS
who had bullied him in Daehangno. The group, Crew Something or Other, had just returned from winning first prize in an international b-boy competition in Germany. They were guests on a talk show, and their excitement was still at a peak. The host kept repeating that the competition was the World Cup of b-boy competitions, dropping mentions of "Korea" and "our people" as he spoke.

He mostly emphasized the last round, a face-off between their team and the Americans. At one point, as he talked about the climax of the match, a sentimental symphonic melody started up and the Korean national flag filled the screen. Jae realized why the b-boys had pushed him out of Daehangno the year before. He was too different from them. He didn't have a spectacular homecoming dream like they did, and he lacked a place he could call home — or anyone to welcome him — so he didn't need fancy clothes or medals. He didn't have fantasies of hard-won success. What Jae had instead was a vague sense of mission, though this energy inside him hadn't yet found the means or the right time to emerge.

For the first time in ages, Jae returned to Daehangno. He didn't see the b-boys he'd met before, but he did see other b-boys practicing on an open stage. There was no sign of Mokran either.

Jae went to the café where he'd heard she was working. He

strode down the stairs and headed straight for the cube so no one had time to stop him. Mokran, lying inside the cube, didn't recognize him right away, not until he breathed onto the clear acrylic wall and drew a J on the fogged-up surface. Their eyes met. He pushed the cube with both hands and it gave easily. The cube's fragility shocked the bystanders, for it had resembled an object from a sci-fi movie, an impenetrable planet surrounded by a strong magnetic field.

The surprised employees dragged Jae away, though he didn't resist, even when the café owner repeatedly punched him in the chin. Mokran rose from the collapsed cube as if bewitched, and followed as they took Jae away. The owner and his employee pulled Jae upstairs by the waist of his pants and waited for the police to arrive.

Only then did Mokran intervene. She said to the café owner, "I'll say you work in the prostitution business."

The owner was silenced by her sudden attack, but the other employee spoke up. "Do you know what happens if you falsely accuse an innocent person?"

"What's 'falsely accuse'?" Mokran said sarcastically. "Is it something you can eat?"

The café owner looked from Jae to Mokran in disbelief. "Is this homeless asshole your boyfriend?"

Mokran glanced at her cell phone. "The police should be here any minute. It takes the 112 patrol cars about five minutes, you know. You could end up on the nine o'clock news. People always believe what they want to believe."

"You bitch!" he said. "What the hell do you want?"

She pointed at Jae. "Let him go."

"If you come back for your paycheck, I'll kill you."

With that, he released Jae.

Mokran got her motorcycle, then drove back so Jae could get on behind her. He didn't care that a wad of the owner's spit landed on his back; his clothes were filthy anyway. They headed toward the Han River.

When they arrived at the riverbank, Mokran asked, "How'd you know I was there?"

"I ran into Donggyu."

She looked up at Jae, intrigued. His face was unwashed, grubby, but his eyes glimmered. They mesmerized her.

"You're pretty tough," she said. "Coming into a stranger's shop and causing hell."

"Nothing ever truly belongs to anyone. Being an owner doesn't mean anything. And anyway, you were locked up in the cube. The cube didn't want that, either."

"That's not it," she said. "I was making money. Going in the cube was my choice."

"I heard the cube's voice as I was coming down the stairs. It said it was ashamed."

"You really hear strange voices coming from nowhere?"

"I know if I say things like that, I'll be hauled off to a mental hospital, but I'm not schizo. The voices I hear don't scare me or anything like that. I just talk to them."

"That's insane."

"I'm not asking you to understand. But I definitely heard its voice."

"So you weren't trying to rescue me, but trying to rescue the cube?"

"I saw you when I got close to the cube. That's when I started getting chest pains again."

"You felt sorry for me? It's not like I was imprisoned or any-thing."

"You're not meant for that place. What I mean is, it's unnat-ural for you to be inside there. Right here, like this, this is more you. There's the river and the wind blowing. The wind's lifting your hair, and it's like the sun's rays are shining down through the strands. It's beautiful. You in front of me this way, it'll prob-ably be one of the last scenes that will come to me right before I die. But that cube in the basement wasn't right for you at all — that's why it was wailing."

"So why haven't I heard it before?"

"Because your senses are broken."

"What senses?" she said. "I'm perfectly fine."

"They say that the Native Americans pleaded for forgiveness from trees before cutting them down. They understood what it meant for a tree to disappear. In asking the trees for forgiveness, they were able to cope with the trees' absence. Cutting down a tree that they'd spent their entire lives looking at was no dif-ferent from cutting off a part of themselves. They didn't have any concept of money — they were directly connected to the ob-jects around them. The act of accepting money to work blocked you from your own awareness. That's why you couldn't hear the cube."

"I don't understand a word you're saying."

"Let yourself open up and take a good look around you," he said. "Don't believe all the clichés. That's the only way to save yourself, because you're worth it."

Jae's last sentence reminded Mokran of a famous makeup advertisement, so she giggled. Jae looked confused, and she re-alized that he didn't know the ad.

Thrown off, she said, "You don't know that ad, do you? 'Because you're worth it.'"

"No."

She grabbed his hand. His hand was warm. "How do you like my bike? Does it suit me?"

"What do you think?"

"I like it. It's comfortable. I think it's right for me."

Jae looked at her solemnly. "Your bike likes you too."

20

JAE WENT ABOUT MEETING PEOPLE IN THIS MAN-
ner. As he had with Mokran and me, he showed up and surprised them. First, he tracked down Hoodie, who was working
as a pizza delivery boy.

The first thing Hoodie said after he opened the door was "If
I don't deliver pizza in thirty minutes, I've got to pay for it." He
stank.

"That's shitty."

"Some customers won't open the door on purpose, just so we
lose thirty minutes."

"Assholes."

Hoodie added, "My sister crept back home, but we've got
enough room to put you up."

Next Jae ran into Baseball Cap on the street. Baseball Cap,
who hadn't outgrown his youthful looks, didn't recognize Jae
since he had shot up over twenty centimeters in a year and
looked a lot older. Plus, he didn't dress like kids his age.

Only when Jae said, "I smashed you up with a beer bottle, remember?" did Baseball Cap realize that it was the "slave." They
had a cigarette together. Baseball Cap was also getting by as a delivery boy at one of the ubiquitous fried chicken fast-food fran-
chises.

As if muttering a curse, Baseball Cap kept repeating,
"Chicken. Our store's chicken is great. Really, it's great."

Jae also visited the house where Hanna had been trapped and tortured. An ordinary family had moved in. When he visited the local corner store and asked about the boys, he learned that they had been shipped to reform school. No one had heard about Geumhui. Jae next headed for where Hanna and her father were said to live and discovered that within a year, Hanna's belly had swelled up like a hill. She still cried and said that she was in love with Leader. Jae felt his heart ripping to pieces as he left.

Jae gave each of them a clear, simple message: "You are all living in the wrong place in the wrong way. It's not your fault, but I feel so much pain because of you." The kids sensed that Jae identified with their suffering, and felt awed by his way of life.

Jae's actions at the time recall those of a martial arts film character who had returned after finishing a long period of training in the mountains. He fearlessly met people, and his confidence and his eccentric looks made a deep impression on his peers. It didn't happen often, but sometimes dozens of kids would circle around Jae to hear him speak. Most were runaways or had quit school, but now and then a perfectly normal school kid would show up.

When I ran into Mokran at one of these gatherings, she asked me, "Don't they look like a bunch of stray cats in a park at midnight?"

I agreed. "It's like watching cats at a rally, nodding off, grooming each other, then slinking away."

Jae walked the entire city and found whatever he required on the spot. He easily picked the locks of donation containers and took whatever clothes and shoes he needed. If necessary, he stole without flinching, for his ideas about ownership were unusual.

Because he was able to communicate with objects, he believed that so long as he respected the object's wishes, there was nothing wrong with taking it and using it for a while. At the same time, he stayed true to his own complex taboos. He avoided the color red because he believed that red symbolized pain and bad luck. He avoided it all: red shirts, beef, bloodshot eyes, and Red Cross blood donation trucks. Whenever he picked up a book, he always ripped out its first and last pages and began reading from the second page. He said that authors had planted something in the first and last page to draw you in. As a result, no one could ever properly read a book that he had finished, and so he became the final reader of every book that he touched.

He also placed great importance on numbers. If the license plate numbers of the first car he saw in the morning added up to a number that ended in a 4, he retreated and did nothing for the entire day. Numbers that came in integers of three — 3, 6, 9, and 15 — were holy. He made exceptions for 12 and 24, since they were common multiples of 4.

One by one, the number of kids spellbound by Jae's odd ways grew. The first time they laughed; the second, they approached him; the third, they paid attention. Then, silently, they began following him.

21

NO MATTER WHAT PEOPLE SAY, MY RUNNING AWAY from home had nothing to do with Jae. But no matter how often I explained myself, I was seen as "the guy who left home to follow Jae."

My stepmom's cold, biased treatment of me was a trite, overplayed story. If a life were only a single volume, maybe mine would have ended there. But despite all the banal stories, life continues. The two girls that came along with my stepmother acted as if they had seen a zombie each time they saw me, and hid behind her skirt. Our mutual hatred and suspicion continued to grow.

The end arose out of nowhere. The night my father was on a stakeout, robbers broke into our house. The men, their faces obscured by masks, climbed across our neighbor's roof and into our home. After they threatened my stepmother, they seized her jewelry, cash, and bottles of liquor, then calmly left. If I had been home, they would have considered the robbery an unavoidable disaster. But that night, I was with Jae and Mokran. Around that time I thought I'd lose it if a day passed and I didn't see her. But if I wanted to see her, I had to be with Jae. When I returned home that day around dawn, the house was bright with lights as if filled with mourners paying their respects.

I was taking my shoes off at the door when my father slapped me across the cheek.

"Why didn't you answer your phone?" he said. "Do you have any idea what time it is? Where the hell have you been?"

My stepmother and her kids were sitting on the couch, staring at me. My father dragged me into the bedroom and began interrogating me. My stepmother must have believed that even if I hadn't been directly involved, I'd had a hand in the robbery. The thieves, as she explained to my father, had sounded as if they had just passed puberty.

She said, "He comes home late every night and won't say a word about where he's gone. Something's fishy about it. I think he's spending time with the wrong crowd."

If I wanted to shake off my father's suspicions, I had hanging out with Jae as my alibi. But I didn't want to tell him. My father was the kind of man who assumed everyone was a potential criminal. If I told him about Jae's life, his suspicions would only be confirmed. From the perspective of a cop, there wasn't a more likely crime suspect than a homeless seventeen-year-old orphan.

I said, "Do you think I did it?"

My father gazed sharply at me, but he didn't go further than that. "Who said I thought you did it?"

"Why're you questioning me like I'm a suspect?"

"Is it strange for a father to ask his son where he's been, when he comes home at four in the morning?"

"Because of all days it's on the day a robber breaks in."

"That's right, I'm glad you brought it up," my father said. "Where were you tonight, of all nights, when a robber broke into the house? You're the eldest son in this house, and we have three women — you're supposed to protect them." ·

"They've got nothing to do with me. And isn't protecting them your job, Father?"

"You really want to take it this far?"

"Can I go to bed now?"

"Then tell me this: Who were you with all this time?"

"I was with a girl."

"A girl?"

"Yes."

He looked at me in disbelief. It was hard to tell whether he couldn't believe I'd slept with a girl, or if he couldn't believe I had just straight-out confessed this to him.

"You trying to show me that you're all grown-up? Saying you're going to live whatever way you want, and that we should leave you alone?"

"I didn't say that."

"It's obvious what kind of girl she is, if she'll stay out all night with a man."

I wanted to say: You act like you know what's up, but you didn't even know that your wife fooled around with your younger brother. I managed to keep the words down and, luckily, my short silence was interpreted as obedience.

"Go to bed," he commanded. "Don't forget that from now on, I've got my eye on you. I've spent my whole life learning that men and animals are nearly the same thing. If you come home this late one more time, I'll lock you out."

My stepmother's anxiety — that worse would happen if I left home — and my father's shame — in not being able to prevent the break-in despite being a cop — turned the house upside down. The original sin was that my father had ignored my stepmother's wish to install an alarm system. As for me, I was shocked that someone could take me for a potential criminal. I hadn't realized just how much my stepmother mistrusted me.

The next day when I told Jae what happened, he said, "Stay with me for a few days." So I did.

He was sleeping in a few different locations — alternating between them. Mokran was staying at a friend's house where Jae could occasionally crash. In addition, there were five or six other places where he slept. Most often, he ended up at a gas station lounge, a room off a Chinese restaurant, or a shelter run by a church. And, more frequently, girls who lived alone let him sleep over.

When I decided not to return home, he encouraged me. "Good decision. Even if it took you a while."

At first I thought that Jae was backing me, but I began having doubts. Mokran sat at his feet, gazing up reverently at him as he offered up radical solutions for my problems. To Mokran, who had lived a pretty sheltered life, since her father was a movie producer, Jae was the essence of cool. Though Jae's difficult past was unimaginable to her, he had quickly become a full-grown man with a unique worldview, and though she had met b-boys and many other types of men, she had never met anyone like him.

He said, "Siddhartha also left home as a teenager."

"Siddhartha? Who's that?" Mokran asked.

"Buddha."

"So Buddha was a person first?"

"He was once a teenager, like us. He was even married."

Mokran was filled with awe. Of course I knew that Jae had been abandoned twice and had led a rough life, and he had read more widely and pondered things more deeply than me. But the advice he casually offered me seemed to diminish what seemed to me the crisis of my very existence. To Jae, all my problems were "no big deal." My parents getting divorced, my father re-marrying a woman who came with her two girls, and her suspi-cions of me — he treated all this as little more than a trite drama you could watch anytime on TV. To him, escaping my situation was simple. He once explained my position to me with a meta-phor: "When you raise an elephant tied up, it won't attempt to leave even if it has the ability. The elephant doesn't know its own strength."

According to Jae I was strong enough but had stupidly been tied to the halter called family, no different from the elephant. Mokran marveled at the clichéd comparison and looked in awe at him. Jae's reading mainly came from whatever he found in recycling bins, so it wasn't exactly orderly or systematic. His dra-matic speeches were steeped in mixed-up maxims from self-help books, religious teachings, and over-the-top heroic phrases from popular fiction. When Jae spoke about other people's lives or about society, nothing he said bothered me. But when it was about my life, I suddenly realized how meaningless his words were. The urgent issues surrounding my family degenerated into trivialities. Maybe Jae was even right. Or maybe my pa-thetic way with words limited Jae's imagination — when I spoke, all my family's pressing problems became just one more mun-dane story. I had thought that at least Jae would be different, but he no longer tried to read my inner thoughts and was still some-how confident that he knew me better than anyone else. This made him even more arrogant.

Mokran acted as if she sympathized with me, but at heart

she was indifferent. To her, I was an excessively ordinary model student who didn't suit someone like Jae. I wasn't actually a brilliant student either, so I was just a nobody who had happened to be Jae's childhood friend. Whenever Jae tossed solutions my way that appeared perfectly clear-cut, I felt humiliated — like a commoner seeking aid from a powerful man. Years later, I saw *The Godfather* on cable TV, and in one scene Marlon Brando asks someone seeking his help, "Why didn't you come to me first?" I immediately thought of Jae. But the reproach lurking behind Jae's bravado was probably aimed more at the world than at me.

To Mokran, I probably seemed like someone who pestered Jae with my small problems, but then hesitated when he gave me invaluable advice. She assumed I wasn't able to accept his straightforward solutions because I was an indecisive person. Still, I didn't lose hope in him, but Jae ended up disappointing me. Just as when we were young, I had faith that he would be sympathetic and understanding. That was why I continued trying to explain what I was going through, but the more I explained, the more unclear and repetitious I became, unable to truly communicate because my words only moved between meaningless complaining and whining. Finally Jae stood up, looking a little bored.

"Let's go," he said.

He took me to a fried chicken joint where two boys he knew ate and slept. "These two'll help you out," he said.

When he knocked on the door, the two boys rushed out. He explained my situation to them, pushed me into the room, then got on the Kawasaki with Mokran and zoomed off.

As soon as I entered the room, a piercing smell hit me. I

recognized it immediately — it was the stench from the waiters' lodgings in Mama Pig's hostess club. The floor was cluttered with a netbook and a TV, and a small fridge lay on a nylon blanket riddled with cigarette holes.

"How do you know Jae?" I asked.

A small kid pointed at the back of his head. "The asshole got me right here with a beer bottle. My hair's long so it covers it, but if you look close you'll see the stitches. So, what are you good for?"

When I hesitated, he asked again. "How are you on a bike? You have a driver's license?"

"No."

"You have any money?"

"Not really."

"You go around chewing uncooked rice too?"

"No."

"Then what the hell were you thinking when you left home?"

I didn't answer.

"Since Jae asked, we'll let you stay here for now. We'll work it out with the owner. He's not rich enough to use another part-timer, but you can run some errands and if there's some fried chicken being tossed out, you can have it."

Early that morning while lying beside the two boys, I was suddenly disturbed by the thought that Jae and I could never be one again. We were becoming complete strangers to each other.

Days later, after my father had my text messages tracked, I was dragged home. But less than a month went by before I ran away again. I was caught once more and sent home, and then I ran away again.

My father said, "Policemen hate repeaters. Meaning, they really detest people who repeat the same crime. Repeat criminals sometimes get stiffer sentences than murderers. The law is stubborn and cruel. My job's to enforce it, but I don't want to do that at home. It's impossible, anyway. In this day and age, the only thing possible for the head of a family is to give up. Don't make your father give up on you."

"I wish you would give up on me," I said.

Meanwhile I got my motorcycle license. I began delivering pizza and earning a little money. It didn't happen as often as before, but after the final delivery on any given night, I would meet up with Jae and Mokran. I bought a prepaid cell phone, and was convinced I was giving my father the slip. More likely, though, my father had given up and was no longer pursuing me. In any case, after months of repeatedly running away and being forced home by my father, I was finally completely free of him.

22

IN THE SPRING, THE MOTORCYCLE GANGS GATHER

under Wonhyo Bridge or around the Yeoido riverfront. On one of those spring days Mokran picked up Jae and headed for the bridge.

"What's around there?" he asked.

"The biker gangs," she replied.

"Why do they hang out there?"

"Some volunteers give them free advice."

"So the crews go there to get help?"

"Of course not."

"Then what?"

"They give them instant noodles," she said. "At first they started to go for the noodles, and after a while, it became a kind of meeting point for them. You know people like going where the crowds are."

It was nearly midnight when kids started showing up. The motorcycles that gathered under the bridge were a diverse group. Beyond the pricey Harley-Davidsons and BMWs, there were ramped-up cheaper models, and even bikes with pizza-chain logos and delivery boxes attached to them.

I joined them on my delivery bike. Jae was wearing a black wool coat that hung loosely from him, so I commented, "You shooting *The Matrix*?"

Jae just grinned. Mokran was in skinny jeans and a flimsy cardigan.

"Aren't you cold?" I asked.

Mokran pouted. "You're always talking about the cold, like an old man."

Some kids approached her, said hello, and left. Jae, who was standing beside her, also got their attention. The riders were smoking in teams, like soldiers about to go to war. Girls hoping for a ride were wandering around in groups of four or five. When the girls saw Mokran, they tried to stay out of her way.

Jae said, "I'll take a quick look around and come back."

He kept a safe distance as he roamed around the groups, which kept up their guard by giving him fierce glances. The motorcycles were huddled together, making guttural growls like wounded animals. Sometimes rock music or hip-hop blasted from a woofer at high volume. There were even kids who spat generous globs at Jae as he approached.

Much later, Jae recalled, "I felt like the kids had been waiting for me. They were snarling like a pack of dogs, but it was as if they were about to lower their tails and accept me if only I came closer. I also heard a voice. It told me: Join them and become one. Lead them and take them somewhere greater. Something like that."

He knew that the hundreds of two-cylinder combustion engines assembled under the bridge were just as excited as their young drivers. Like cavalry horses mounted for war, they heaved as if eager to gallop ahead. Most of all, Jae fervently desired to communicate with these impulsive machines. If only he could drive on one of them, he would be more intimate with them and his body would become a machine, and the machine, his body. He felt as if he had been transformed again into the burning scooter when the dogs had run free.

After midnight the mood around Wonhyo Bridge became wilder. One group made deafening noises as they headed downtown, and other groups followed. Kids killing time by filling out a local government survey also returned to their motorcycles, and one by one, revved up their engines.

The volunteers saw them off, yelling, "Be careful."

The kids waved goodbye with the light wands in their hands.

Three or four groups headed for the city center first. The girls shrieked and egged on the boys gripping the bike's handles. Other groups who had taken in the situation texted each other and began lining up. No one wore helmets. As excitement continued to build, yet another group, one with over thirty members, descended and settled under Wonhyo Bridge. The rest of the first group about to leave halted and faced the new group, as if receiving guests. There were no streetlights around them, so it was much darker than the park with the volunteers, and only their high-beam lights revealed their faces. Like bees buzzing around a beehive, dozens of motorcycles circled around the parked ones.

Jae stepped out and gazed out at the bikes. The loitering girls clambered onto any bike with an empty backseat. Jae paid special attention to the flashiest bike in the middle of the group.

Mokran said, "That's Taeju's group."

Jae asked, "Who's Taeju?"

"He's the leader of the coolest biker gang. Also my ex-boyfriend."

As if submitting to a military inspection, Taeju's group made a large circle beneath the bridge. As soon as Taeju spotted Mokran, he stopped his bike.

"How've you been?" he asked.

"Not bad."

"Who's the homeless guy beside you?"

Taeju looked hard at Jae. Jae didn't look away.

She said, "Siddhartha."

"Who's Siddhartha?"

"Just someone."

Taeju turned toward the ramp. After absorbing the rest of the remaining bikes, the enormous procession began heading toward the Gangbyeon Expressway. The roaring engines and flashy lights suddenly disappeared and Wonhyo Bridge became more desolate. Some volunteers packed up. Others said they would stay until sunrise and keep watch. As for me, I was looking at Jae. His soul was seeking another tower made of crates of whiskey, a lonely tower that he could climb up to gaze out at the world that had abandoned him. In the end that tower would collapse, and again, I would witness the fall.

23

THAT APRIL, IN THE FULL BLOOM OF CHERRY BLOS-
soms, we raced over the scattered petals under the streetlights.
At the time, it was just the three of us, Jae, me, and Mokran.

While eating ice cream under a cherry blossom tree, I said to
Jae, "That smell, I can smell it on you."

"What smell?"

"You know, Mama Pig's hostess club. The waiters' lounge."

In other words, the smell of poverty — the stink of fish coming from young men sharing a room.

"As if you don't smell," said Mokran. She started the engine.
"Let's hit the road."

Jae and Mokran sped across the bank of the Han River, falling back then moving ahead of each other. They rode gently
then forcefully, like a veteran ice-dancing couple gliding across
the rink. I wedged myself between them, but they quickly became one again.

Though Jae had started riding later than we had, he was the
fastest. Mokran didn't like motorcycles for what they were; for
her, they were merely a way to socialize. Since Taeju, her ex,
had essentially lived on one, she learned to ride to be with him.
I wasn't skilled, but I thrived on pure speed. According to Jae, I
had an aggressive driving style. But Jae, he literally became one
with his motorcycle. At a certain point while racing ahead of us,
he'd forget our very existence.

When Mokran mentioned this, Jae nodded. "You're right. That's exactly it. It's hard to explain. But the bike and I becoming one — well — it's not really that. My mind begins permeating the bike. Inside it, I think, look out at the world, and keep moving."

Jae told us about mysterious experiences he'd started having while in solitary confinement, but we didn't really believe him. We just assumed they were moments when he'd gone a bit mad. This was a little before Jae displayed the kind of masterful driving skills that he would soon show us. He was beginning to develop a driving style of his own, which was bold and elegant, and the biker groups had started to notice.

He asked us, "Have you ever been to the beach?"

I knew for sure that Jae had never been to the beach. The word "vacation" didn't exist in Mama Pig's vocabulary.

"What about you?" Mokran asked.

"Jeongeun said we should come over," he said.

Jeongeun used to hang out with Jae until he broke his leg while delivering pizza on a rainy day. With the "thirty-minute promise of delivery" or whatever they call it, pizza delivery had turned into a life-or-death race against time. Only some time after his accident did Jeongeun finally tell everyone that he was staying in a village near the West Sea. He could no longer support himself, so he had returned to the seaside where his grandmother lived.

Mokran settled onto the bike seat. "Why not take off and go now?"

"This late at night?" I asked.

Mokran insisted. "Why not? We can drive up again in the morning. Only two hours and we'll be there."

The three of us took a local road. Freight trucks, steered by drivers on stimulants to stay awake, stumbled over the center-line. We ignored traffic lights and raced southwest, and only when we reached the bridge connecting the mainland to the island did we turn off our ignition switches and cool the engines. The black sea was glossy and gleamed under the streetlights, and Mokran's long hair fluttered in the wind. I liked looking at her; it was as if she had been created from all the good things of the world. Our eyes kept meeting; she knew that I was watching her.

Jae said, "It's the ocean!" He began running toward it and threw himself into the water. Mokran followed.

"Oh, my shoes, my shoes!" he said. His slipper had come off while he was wading.

The water was cold and the ocean at night was inky black, desolation itself, but we laughed and shoved each other. We hunted for Jae's slipper while splashing and having water fights. Finally Mokran raised the slipper high above her head, like a trophy, and said, "I found it!"

Jae swung an arm over Mokran's shoulder and suddenly kissed her on the cheek. I walked along the dark beach. Jae, now out of the water, lit a cigarette as I watched Mokran.

I heard an engine approaching from the distance. It was Jeongeun's younger brother, who was only fourteen and already riding a 500cc scooter. "It's common in the country," he told us.

We followed him down a rural road. A chill I hadn't felt before when at the beach tightened around me. Jeongeun's grandmother, an early riser, was already up. She looked indifferently at us as if we were local mutts passing through. She seemed like a person who had long ago quit making judgments about the world. Jeongeun then emerged sleepily on crutches. After he'd affectionately greeted and cursed Jae, he welcomed Mokran and me. We had warm water a few minutes after the boiler was turned on, so we took turns showering, starting with Mokran.

Early the next morning, we had the breakfast that Jeongeun's grandmother prepared and headed out to the sea again. We went down a road cut into a hill until we were suddenly faced with the vast ocean. Jae was briefly reduced to silence. Mokran and Jeongeun, and me seated behind Jae, stayed quiet. We turned the engines off and stopped talking, and forgot about one another.

Finally Jae spoke. "There's nothing here."

Mokran, who every summer had visited several beaches within the country and beyond, said, "What else is there in the ocean except the ocean?"

As if defending the ocean, Jeongeun replied, "Well, it's not high season yet. And there's a ton of stuff in the ocean. The clams alone . . ."

But Jae had immediately perceived the ocean's strangeness. The ocean was the vastness of nothing. He thought of a past when he had not existed and the future when he wouldn't exist, and felt something close to terror. It was as if cosmic time, without beginning or end, had been transformed into the ocean and appeared in front of him.

24

MOTORCYCLE RALLIES TOOK PLACE EVERY WEEK-
end, and our idyllic night drives quickly came to an end. If
Jae showed up, the numbers jumped. There were many nights
when close to a hundred bikes snaked through the city, and dozens of kids who stayed after the drives stuck close to Jae. My position within the circle was uncertain. His new followers were
tough and clearly looked down on me, so I was overwhelmed
with gratitude whenever Jae paid me any attention, and at the
same time I despised myself. The kids noticed me when Jae ad-
dressed me, and then would forget about me again.

Every weekend Jae lived like a king: a king in shorts and
cheap slippers. But that was the style in this crowd. You had to
wear shorts until your knees were scarred up, and you had to go
without a helmet until you busted your head in. Young cocks
puffed out their chests and paraded their courage — all a show
that scoffed at the possibility of dying. But the kids weren't old
enough to know the difference between show and insanity. That
was why they crowned mad Jae their king.

The higher Jae rose, the lower I fell. I felt as if I'd been the
king's eunuch all my life. Even though I knew a lot about the
king, I couldn't freely divulge information about him. Even if
the kids spread completely ridiculous rumors about Jae, I kept
my mouth shut. Of course I wanted to set the facts straight, but
it was obvious that it would be seen as trying to climb the ranks

by parading my friendship with Jae. Besides, Jae seemed to enjoy the rumors.

Was it like the just-hatched sea turtle that finally reaches the ocean? For Jae's true character began to slowly emerge and reveal itself. I quickly realized that popularity is power, and power the ability to achieve what violence seeks to achieve, but without violence. He was cruel to those who challenged him and gentle to those who followed. He executed orders with one glance. Those who challenged him were either kicked out or found themselves in real trouble. It ultimately led to Jae's crew being more organized than any other. Loyalty to Jae wasn't necessarily fostered by resorting to violence, for his way of confronting the police was unique. Though groups before him had scattered and fled at the sight of a patrol car and regrouped later, Jae would block the advance of patrol cars or breach their defense altogether.

The police weren't prepared for motorcycle gangs that openly attacked them. Those Jae led felt thrilled and proud; it made them think they were different from the others, which led them to adore their leader. Sometimes he'd have several patrol cars chasing him while he was alone and he'd still elude them, or he'd hide in an alley and suddenly speed ahead and ambush them. Thanks to Jae, the kids realized that the patrol cops didn't have the nerve to ram into their bikes and were only intent on preventing accidents. Teenagers in slippers who lacked helmets and knee guards endlessly played with the cops, who were equipped with all sorts of gear. In the daytime the police force was king; the sight of a cop alone made the delivery boys cower. The cops grinned while slapping them with fines for trivial violations like riding without a helmet and running traffic lights, and some cops even cuffed them affectionately on the head or pulled at their ears. But at night the cops were sitting ducks. The kids who docilely accepted traffic tickets during the day stormed the cops at night, like zombies hungry for blood.

Jae once said, "They think we speed to relieve stress? It's not stress. Are you stressed when a storeowner hits you over the head with a metal tray? Are you stressed when you make a delivery to a wrong address, then spot some assholes who've played with you, looking down from a window and laughing? Are you stressed when cops catch you as easy prey to fill their quota, talking down to you while writing you a ticket? No, you're stressed when you've got an exam tomorrow and haven't studied, or you're late meeting someone and the roads are jam-packed. That's when you feel stressed. So what is it we're feeling?

"It's rage. Shit, it's fucking rage. That's right, we're so angry, we drive because we're so pissed off, and what're we angry about? About this fucked-up world. What's the meaning of the root *pok* in *pokju*? The root's meaning is 'violence.' If you're well behaved, you're not a biker. Only when we make a lot of noise, smash up signs, and bring traffic to a dead stop will the world notice us. Racing's the way we let them know we're angry. How? With fucking violence. Can't we just talk to them? No. Why? 'Cause we're no good with words. Because words belong to old people. They know they'll win with words, so that's why they keep telling us to talk to them."

I cautiously disagreed. "You think the world will understand us? When we're waking them up at night, blocking the roads, and smashing everything up?"

"I'm not trying to get them to understand. I'm trying to piss them off. The world hates us 'cause they're fucking jealous.

They'd feel comfortable if we stayed crushed — making deliveries and studying for the high school certificate exam — but here we are, ignoring traffic lights and lanes and racing wherever we like, and not going home till late. We're riding with young girls on our backseats that old men drool over. So yeah, they wanna kill us. You think they don't understand us? No, they get us. That's why they hate us."

"You're saying you want everyone to know we're angry?"

"There's something I learned at the home. There's a ton of kids there and few grownups. If you hit someone, one of the grownups shows up and asks, 'Why'd you hit him?' I used to think that was their way of communicating and caring about us. But I realized that they just ask, and later, they still punish. But the world's punishing us anyway. Take a look at the wrecks I lead. If they're not being punished, who is? They wake up at dawn and go to work, they're cursed at and treated bad, get looked down on, risk their lives making deliveries whether it rains or snows, work without any days off."

My life epitomized what Jae was talking about. If I so much as smelled pizza, I would feel like throwing up. I went to bed exhausted every night, wondering if I should go back home and return to school. But even if I did, at most I had two years left after returning to the fenced-in area that passed itself off as a family. With my grades the chances of going to a good university were slim to start with, so returning to school meant little. But I wasn't satisfied with my present life either. A penniless teenager was worthless and earned the same wages as an illegal worker. These kids, receiving the minimum wage, put up with the worst treatment; with no way to protest, most had no idea that they were being treated like animals.

I said, "But society's different from school or the orphanage 'cause the punishments never stop. You can end up an outsider forever."

"That's how it usually happens," he said. "But I'm different. I'll be different. Just watch."

Jae would always look at me as if he were a teacher gazing down at a student who lacked faith. Each time his eyes met mine I had the sense that he had suddenly "discovered" me. At dawn one day after we finished speeding through the city, Jae suddenly asked me, "What's this? You're still here?"

Since Jae was the boss and the kids laughed at anything he said, they laughed when he shot this my way. The number of times I had to decide whether to laugh with the others or get angry increased. If you couldn't laugh with the others, you became the odd one out. Even so, I continued to watch Jae. I'd always believed that the word "I," reflected in the mirror, was actually Jae. The left and the right could be reversed, but they were fundamentally the same, like Siamese twins, only older and separated.

Once, when I was imprisoned by words, we had been one. If I thought something, Jae said it and acted it for me. Later, before I'd even formed the thought, Jae spoke and acted ahead of time for me. Even when I overcame aphonia and began speaking, our relationship stayed constant. Though we had lived apart for years, as soon as Jae returned, we reverted to our old ways. Whatever I imagined, Jae had always put it immediately into action.

Leaving home and drifting, meeting Mokran and falling in love, leading the ranks of motorcycles to speed across the city, Jae had done it all. I was always the one lagging behind, watching him.

Different. Jae had said he was different. I asked him, "What do you mean, you're different?"

Jae said, "An image came to me. It's hard to describe, but it's becoming clearer and clearer. Remember learning calligraphy in third grade, in an elective class? Do you remember our calligraphy teacher, the one with the white beard?"

I nodded. As soon as the teacher had entered class, he had immediately done a demonstration in front of the kids. With a thick brush he made a downward stroke, continued in a precariously thin line, then arced until he gently returned, finishing the letter. The incomprehensible words resembled a painting, and the teacher's way with the brush, a dance.

Jae asked again, "Do you remember the bearded guy? 'The moment your brush touches the paper, you must never hesitate or stop. You've got to keep to the original path you had in mind.'"

For Jae, speed was an artistic experience. Riding the motorcycle was like taking a thick, powerful brush to the city streets, even if no one understood what he was writing.

He said, "Imagine if I wasn't the only one taking a brush to the streets, but that thousands, tens of thousands of others were doing it too. That's the painting I'm seeing."

25

JAE BEGAN LEAVING MOKRAN AND ME BEHIND MORE

often. She was officially his girlfriend, but because of her connection to the past, Jae saw us as having the same ambiguous, indefinable rank. And as soon as Jae began ignoring us, we both became nonexistent.

Mokran lit a cigarette. "I don't think Jae likes me riding."

"Why?"

"You know I beat the girls up."

Mokran hated the girls who clamored for a ride. She wasn't the only one — most of the girls who raced with the group on their own motorcycles felt that way. When Mokran showed up, the girls crept away. The guys who rode with Jae weren't exactly pleased with this. I once saw Mokran have a go at one of the girls. She slapped the girl's cheek fast and hard. The girl glared at Mokran, but she didn't dare fight back and Mokran kept slapping until the girl looked away.

"Why don't you just ride with Jae?" I asked her.

"Should I? No, I'd hate that. That's so humiliating."

Her leg shook furiously as she spoke. At that time, Jae had quietly started messing around with other girls, so her nerves were shot.

"Are all guys like that?" she asked.

A cruise ship glided down the river, and evening strollers detoured around us. Mokran tossed the cigarette butt toward the water, and the tiny light flew through the air and disappeared. The fluorescent streetlights turned her hands blue.

"You would know that better than I do, wouldn't you?"

"So you think that too, that I know guys real well."

"I didn't mean it that way. I just meant I don't really know either."

"Jae's weird, but you're pretty weird too. Why're you in this biker gang anyway? You don't seem the type."

"What type do I seem?"

Mokran gazed directly at me. It was the first time she'd truly seen me as a human being, and I had to look away. "Anyway," she said, "this kind of place doesn't suit you."

"And?"

"I don't know. First, you hardly speak. And you don't seem interested in girls, and you drive carefully. Is it 'cause you like Jae? I mean, do you love him?"

This was her surprise assault. I hadn't ever thought about it. Truthfully, I didn't exactly know what the difference was. More than having feelings for Jae, I felt helplessly joined to him.

"Does it look that way to you?" I asked.

"Why else would you be here? You don't seem like a groupie. You and Jae are just weird. Sometimes it's like you're Jae's shadow, and other times it's like Jae's your shadow."

I remembered how as a kid I'd make shadows when the lights had gone out in the house, my hand becoming a wolf or a rabbit. Maybe Jae was one of the shadows I'd made.

"Actually, one of the girls likes you. Have you noticed?"

I had no idea.

"So you never noticed. Her name's Jonghui, you know, the one with freckles and big eyes."

I didn't actually know the names of any of the girls she hung out with.

"She's into you. You really didn't know?"

"No."

"You aren't interested?"

"No."

"See. You're weird." She looked hard at me again.

I nervously met her eyes for the first time. My head was numb as if I'd eaten red-bean ice flakes too quickly. I lowered my head and abruptly confessed, "Actually . . . I like you."

Mokran didn't really look alarmed. As if to comfort me, she said, "You know I'm practically a whore."

"Don't say that."

In a melancholy voice, she said, "Jae never goes far with me. Did you know that?"

I was so surprised, I asked, "You haven't slept with him yet?"

Jae often shared a room with Mokran. Sometimes there were other kids with them, but it wasn't an issue if Jae wanted it.

She said, "No."

A lot of girls bragged that they had slept with Jae. I'd also seen him come out of the bathroom smoothing out his pants, with a girl following behind. There was plenty of evidence of Jae acting like the big man, so I was surprised that nothing had happened between them.

"I've sucked him off, but he didn't seem to like it so much."

The first time I'd seen Mokran, she'd been the woman coolly lounging in the cube. But now she was hitting rock bottom. On top of that she was dragging Jae down with her. I covered my ears with both hands. "Don't say another word. I don't want to hear it."

"You're the first person I've talked to about this stuff."

Why? Because I was Jae's shadow? Because I was an idiot who wouldn't tell anyone?

"I really don't want to hear it. I told you, I like you."

"If I can't even talk to you, I'll be so frustrated I'll go crazy."

"It's 'cause . . . you're important to Jae."

"No, it's 'cause I'm just a dishrag, or something like that."

"Don't say that. You're really beautiful. I know you're a good person."

"Liar!" she said. "I've been on the streets for years."

Mokran rested her head on my shoulder. I was thrown off as I rested my arm around hers. Our faces were so close, I could instantly smell her cheap face powder. We were so close that if I wanted to, I could have kissed her forehead. No, her lips. But I didn't. I had absolutely no desire to. It was strange. It wasn't because she had dragged herself down. The moment I realized that Jae had never slept with Mokran, all my feelings for her disappeared. I realized I had fallen for her because I'd believed that Jae wanted her.

My penis had gone hard in my tight pants, but it was as if I were standing back and watching the situation. When I did nothing, Mokran swiftly slipped from my arms. As if I'd insulted her, she got on the Kawasaki and left without speaking. I was thinking about Mokran's questions. Why was I here, and what kind of a person was I? The shadow blocking me from the world was Jae. I didn't have any more room for Mokran.

I started thinking of a ridiculous but fundamental solution until I convinced myself it was unavoidable. I quickly got up and paced up and down the riverside. Some drunk people staggered by, cursing confusedly at me before wobbling into the distance. I stared at the columns, bright with dazzling lights, on the bridge over the Han River.

When had I started dreaming about Jae's death? No, that was a cowardly question. For some time, it was clear I'd imagined, even desired, Jae's death. I had played out his death repeatedly in great detail to myself, predicting how mournful I'd be once he was gone. Even worse, I'd imagined that I would be directly involved in his death. Meaning, I had considered murdering him.

Murder is the most extreme form of fantasy. Once you cross that line, you can't experience anything in the same way again. Simply imagining it is enough. Once you become obsessed with murder, you're no longer satisfied with sports or computer games. I began watching movies and reading books involving murder. I wondered whether the idea of "living vicariously" that grownups talked about was possible. It wasn't. Living vicariously. The expression was a lie made up by people who had never fantasized about murder.

Why Jae, of all people? Was I jealous of him? Or was it because of Mokran? Whenever he was in the limelight, or Mokran rested her cheek on his back as if it were the softest of pillows, I felt miserable. But I remember it clearly. That seed didn't first bud from envy; it stemmed from a curiosity about how I would feel if Jae died. The subject of my first fantasies of murder was my uncle. It was probably right after he'd slapped my mother. Then when my father and mother fought, I'd wished for my mother to die. Since my father was almost always out anyway, I thought that with my mother's death the house would finally be quiet. I wanted a house as quiet as a coffin but our house was always noisy. Jae always wanted the opposite, but he was left behind in an abandoned redevelopment area. In this way, Jae's and my circumstances were always at odds.

People talk about sadness. They say that when we lose a family member or someone close to us, we'll feel a deep sense of loss, but I'd never experienced this. And I felt shame for not knowing what this felt like. Let's say there's a balloon filled with water. If the balloon popped, water would explode everywhere, and if it was sadness inside that balloon, my body would be drenched with it. Only then I'd know what the smell of sadness is. But what if I popped the balloon on purpose? Would that sadness still be the same? Would something change? Would my guilt bury the sadness? Would the person who used guilt to replace sadness be a truly strong person?

Sadness or guilt, they were both abstract, lofty emotions to me. I became confused by my desire to experience these emotions. I didn't wait for these emotions to come naturally to me, no, I rejected that from the start. Like a bartender mixing different liquors to make a cocktail, I created the emotions myself, and I wanted to thoroughly experience what I had made according to my plan. The chaos inside me finally led to my murder fantasies. Only when I thought about murder did my anxiety and sense of defeat vanish, the way an approaching typhoon stops birds from twittering.

PART
FOUR

26

WHEN PAK SEUNGTAE'S HARLEY-DAVIDSON NEARED
the police station, growling and spitting smoke into the air, the
station's conscripted policemen saluted him. He parked the bike
in a corner of the parking lot.

"Lieutenant Pak." One of the uniform-clad policemen approached him.

"What is it?"

"The chief of security would like a word with you."

As soon as Pak entered the room, the chief of security stopped
skimming the newspaper and took off his reading glasses. He
said, "Just look at your outfit."

It wasn't the first time Seungtae had to hear this. The man
went after Seungtae each time he saw him in his leather jacket.
Everyone below the chief of police finally just let it go except for
the chief of security, who kept making it an issue.

"Who'd guess you were a government-employed policeman in those clothes?" he said. "They'd think you were part of
a gang."

"Couldn't it help when I'm working undercover? Like cam-
ouflage."

"That's a load of bull. The biker-gang assholes in our country
can't wear these kinds of clothes."

"Why? Too pricey?"

"How could Chink-food delivery boys who work through

downpours wear leather in the rain? A T-shirt from Dongdae-mun Market's more fitting."

The chief of security twirled a pen between his fingers. "When did you make it to lieutenant?"

"It's been three years, sir."

"You've got men working under you, and just look at you. Do they ever do what they're told? I'm telling you this because I worry about you."

Seungtae flushed. "Is there something you needed me to do?"

Like a school principal who had called in a troublemaker, the chief steadily glared at Seungtae without saying anything. Finally he asked, "You still on the motorcycle every night, zipping around?"

"It's not during work hours, so it's not an issue, is it, sir?"

"Why're you wandering outside your jurisdiction? We've got a lone wolf in our station."

"But you're aware of what I'm doing. I'm patrolling for biker gangs."

"On a Harley-Davidson?"

"Yes."

"You in the Traffic Department?"

"Kids are on bikes screeching all over the city center, making a mess, and the local force can't stop them. If a local station sends out a patrol car to subdue them, they hop districts like grasshoppers. We need people exclusively responsible for pursuing and rounding them up."

The chief of security said, "I know. But why're you the one cracking down on them? That's why I'm asking, are you in Traffic or Juvie?"

"I don't directly bust them," said Seungtae. "I've done this work for a long time so I know the kids. I go out and try to reason with them, and if that doesn't work, I pick up a few for the local station, but you're already aware of this."

"Enough. Just don't do it anymore."

"If we leave the situation as it is now, it'll become a social problem."

"What's a lowly lieutenant doing in a panic about social problems and all? Are you a National Assembly rep? Those brats. They roam around for a while then just turn in come dawn. So why're you going wild trying to chase and catch them? Those slippery rascals, they're always out of your reach, and even if you catch them it's only a warning or fine for them. What if someone ends up dead? How're you going to handle the backlash? Do you really want an investigation by the human rights commission, a headquarters inquiry? You think we're backing off like this 'cause we can't keep up, like the American police can? If we send out a chopper, crash into them with our patrol cars, and shoot off net guns, we can get them all, why not? We're already catching wild boars, and you have any idea how sharp they are? If trained, those animals could even do basic arithmetic. I bet the smart ones have a higher IQ than some of these bike-racing shitfaces."

"The public's complaining a lot —"

"Seungtae." The chief of security cut him off.

"Yes?"

"You think there's a single guy in Korea who likes the motorcycle gangs? With the muffler removed, the noise is outrageous. They ride with slutty bitches behind them, they don't give a rat's ass about the centerline, drive the wrong way on the street. If you see them, of course you want to kill them right off. Take a look at the comments online. *What's the use of having fun? Why aren't you using your guns?* It's an outrage. A mess. That's one thing the public agrees on: they all hate them. But if we trust public opinion and tear after the kids, we get turned to shit in the press. You know what I'm saying?"

Seungtae stayed silent.

"Why aren't you saying anything? Are you saying you're still going out there? Your ass must like the media shots of you on the Harley. Like you've become some kind of celebrity, yeah? A cop ought to be in the papers for doing his job well — you think it's okay for a cop to end up in the papers for riding a Harley? I'll give you some advice. If you want to be promoted, you better not pop up in the dailies. You understand me?"

"Yes, sir."

The chief of security looked intently at Seungtae and smirked. " 'Yes, sir?' That's so sincere. Maybe — your heart's with the bikers?"

"Come on, sir . . ."

"I heard you're part of some club."

"Oh, they're a different breed from the teen motorcycle gangs. Our members strictly abide by the traffic laws and —"

"More talking out of your ass! Honestly, I think you're showing off your money. Wait till you get married and have kids and have to send them to school. You won't have that kind of cash. How can a motorcycle cost tens of thousands of dollars? You keep riding one of those and you'll have an inspector on your tail. It's not like your father owns a fancy building in the Gangnam district, right?"

Seungtae stayed silent.

"I'll lay off your hobbies. It's not my business whether you go to Yangsuri or Sokcho on weekends, but I don't want you messing around in someone else's jurisdiction and causing trouble. And I want the criminal stats compiled by the weekend on my desk. You can go now."

Seungtae returned to his desk and hung his jacket on a hanger. He'd slipped a full-length photo of himself from a year-old men's fashion magazine under his desk's glass panel. The project involved short interviews and photos of men who broke job-related stereotypes. A fund manager who played the cello in a string quartet, a junior high school teacher who'd won a Latin dance competition, a lawyer who owned a classical music record store, and others, gathered in a Gangnam basement studio. Seungtae had been labeled "the squad chief night-racing on a Harley-Davidson," though he wasn't exactly a squad chief.

"Bring handcuffs or some other object that shows you're a cop," the photographer's assistant had said.

As requested, Seungtae brought handcuffs and a baton with him. He wore his leather motorcycle jacket and vintage leather boots, and carried the handcuffs in his left hand. He'd come with his hair gelled back, but the photographer didn't seem to like it so he dug through the prop room and brought out a bandana. Seungtae liked the photo. He asked the photographer for the unused stills to frame and hang up at home.

No one who knew him ever thought he would become a cop. As a kid, he had been different from the other boys. He disliked macho sports like soccer and basketball, and was more interested in fashion, art, and music. He tried to fit in with the boys, but was slow to find interests in common with them. He followed the boys to a baseball stadium to watch a pro-league game, but he couldn't say he enjoyed it. In his last year of middle school on a camping trip on Jeju Island, he met a man in his thirties, a supervisor come to help them camp. Seungtae got along well with him, and the man knew it too. One day the man took him aside to a cabin where the supervising teachers usually gathered, and asked him a few questions — a furtive Q & A — from "Do you have a girlfriend?" to "How many times a week do you masturbate?" Seungtae was embarrassed answering these questions, but he wasn't uninterested. The man was kind and he seemed to be gently introducing Seungtae to an unfamiliar world. Then the man leaned in toward him and whispered, "The way it looks to me, you've got to be . . ."

Seungtae, who'd kept his head bowed down as they spoke, finally looked up. Their eyes met.

". . . gay."

Seungtae was shocked. He immediately denied this, and said there was no way he could ever be gay. The man continued. "You've never had a girlfriend, even though you're good-looking, well built, and a good student, but you've never wondered why?"

"I just haven't met the perfect girl yet, that's all."

"You really think that's it?"

Seungtae continued to deny it, but he didn't storm away.

"There's a simple way to find out if you're gay or not."

Seungtae wondered what this method was, and waited for him to keep speaking. Instead of words, the man came to him with his lips and threw his arms around him. Seungtae squirmed. Deep down he worried about what would happen if he were actually gay, so he let the man continue to find out. He definitely felt aroused, and it was the first time he'd felt such sensations, but he'd never been with a woman before, so it was impossible to know for sure.

The man called Seungtae once he returned to Seoul. He wanted to meet. When Seungtae refused, the man threatened that he would tell his parents about their talk and everything that went on between them. After that, he motel-hopped with the man a number of times. He took to thinking deeply and often about whether he was born gay or had become gay because of the man. The more he thought about it, the more he became interested in how he felt about boys his age. He tried hard to break free from the man's net of suggestions. He decided that to do this, he would need to be more masculine and have a body to match, so he began to exercise. He spent two hours a day lifting weights in the apartment complex's gym, and upon entering high school, decided that he would become a professional soldier or a cop. This new Seungtae who wasn't considered gay by any of his family members or friends explored the sexual identity buried deep inside him. He began surfing gay sites, looking for evidence that he wasn't gay, and ended up becoming addicted to those very sites. He became angry at himself. It was as if the world were laughing at his expense.

He concluded that the man he met at the camp was responsible for his unhappiness, and the next time he went to the agreed-upon motel, he punched the man in the face, brought him down, bound him with a pair of toy handcuffs he'd purchased at a store, and beat him with a police baton he'd bought near Yongsan subway station. He took it even further. But when he returned home, he started feeling sorry for the damaged, bruised man and cried.

In a way, it was as if Seungtae had been reborn through the man. To be precise, it was his words that changed Seungtae. The man told him what kind of person he was, but when he tried to move ahead, he couldn't break free from those words. To the new Seungtae, the man he had met at camp was like a father, and by being violent with him he became physically free of him. But that didn't mean he was mentally free of him. The man's very identity became disconnected from its origin, and so was owned solely by Seungtae. He could no longer beat up or kill a father he couldn't see.

Eventually Seungtae became the same age that the supervising teacher at camp had been, complete with a police badge. It was like a magical joker card — he could go anywhere and get complete access. At age thirty, even though he had been with several partners, he realized that he was attracted to teenage boys. Like the camp supervisor, he had the same desire to shape the boys' identities — not so much a desire to cavort with teenage boys, but a desire to flex his power over them. He'd long known that kids like him were easily captivated by a stranger's alluring words. Sometimes when they didn't fall for it, he bullied them with violence and authority, and each time, felt relief. A feeling that he was safe. He was becoming addicted to this feeling.

Seungtae's night starts where the biker crews assemble. He watches them from his Harley. Cheap motorcycles fashioned to make maximum noise; teenagers smoking; kids unaware of who they are, unaware that self-awareness is necessary, but who have an instinctive, brazen desire to shake up the city with explosive noise and speed.

Sometimes he strides between them. He picks the toughest-looking one and approaches him, shows him his officer badge, and forces the kid to his knees. Korean motorcycle gangs are entirely different from those in America or Japan, which are made up of grownups and are part of a real gang. The Korean motorcycle gangs are mainly teenagers, just a fearful group of ragtag kids. They don't sell drugs like the American motorcycle gangs, or start wars against the Yakuza like the Japanese ones. No matter how much they posture, they are, in the end, just kids. They might be dangerous when on the move, but parked and chatting with one another, they are easy to control. These kids don't know their legal rights. They aren't interested in a cop's responsibilities during questioning. Seungtae behaves like a high school principal to these dopey teen gangs who speak to him in grammatically incorrect, respectful sentences. He asks the terrified kids for their school and home addresses and their phone numbers, and the kids answer. He knows that many of the bikes that the kids ride are stolen, but he doesn't dig that deeply. Subtly frightening them is enough to realize his goal. But everything changed once Jae entered the picture.

Frequent rumors about the new guy Jae had begun reaching Seungtae. Jae wasn't yet as powerful as he would become, but he was worth noting. The police still didn't have a single photo of him, but Seungtae wasn't really worried about it. Once a teenager was hauled into the station, he revealed everything, so Jae's whereabouts could easily be confirmed. A large number of the kids that Seungtae encountered knew about Jae. What they said about his place of birth, his appearance, and where he lived was all over the place, but they were united on one thing: he was different from anyone else, and he was still powerful. Seungtae made a folder tagged JAE, tossed it into the file cabinet, and took out a file labeled OH TAEJU. Catching Taeju was his first priority.

27

SEUNGTAE HAD WAITED A LONG TIME FOR A CHANCE
to nab Taeju. Of course if he really wanted to, he could get him
right away and terrify him. He could turn him over to the civil
court for violating traffic laws, and get him sentenced with a
fine and community service. He was only a broke teenager without a lawyer, educated parents, or any clue about human rights
abuses. But what Seungtae wanted was to put the noose around
Taeju once and for all.

Taeju's driving was bold and magnetic. A motorcycle takes
on different styles for different drivers, and Taeju's driving was
like an effortless, dashing cursive. He turned corners smoothly
— at a deep angle, without slowing. Even when patrol cars came
at him from all directions, he wasn't thrown off balance; instead,
he continued to make quick judgments and lead his crew. To do
that required being able to read the police's next move. In the
game that the biker crews had started on the *baduk* board of
the city, victory or defeat depended on this battle of intellect. If
the police force's strategy worked, the crew would break up and
the night would die down.

The general public trusted that the police had pitched camp
in order to arrest the biker crews, but that wasn't true. All the
police did was cut off their tail and slowly drain their strength.
Trying to arrest them would be an expensive, inefficient strategy
for maintaining public peace. The bikers' leader combated this

pressure by trying to maintain the group and continue riding. But an exceptional leader would reattach the tail that the police had cut off and regain strength.

As the police tried one strategy after another to take hold of the situation, the other drivers on the road became only vague obstacles. A large-scale motorcycle rally is like the Crusades. The participating feudal lords and their knights never pledged unconditional fidelity to the king; if something displeased them, they returned to their kingdom. The leader's main role in a large crew made up of smaller crews from the metropolitan area was to command and direct the other bike leaders, but it was impossible to hear anything over the explosive sound blanketing the night streets. The leader's riding skill was his only form of leadership, so his strength plummeted if he wasn't visible.

This was Taeju's weak spot. He was a leader impatient with the slow ones in the back. If the tail was snipped off here and there, he would be left brashly speeding off on his own. By two in the morning this kind of motorcycle rally lost momentum and broke up. The smaller crews that had been cut off inevitably roamed the streets until they were caught in police traps, or parted ways, exhausted.

Recently a snitch that Seungtae had planted came in with an important tip. This kid became a spy after Seungtae smacked him around and threatened to send him to reform school. He had collected a few of these little spies. There was even one kid who turned over an entire list of riders from the previous night's motorcycle rally. In any case, the snitch told him that Taeju had a Yamaha R1 that was stolen from a shop in the Chungmuro neighborhood. The situation was complicated: the shop where the bike had gone missing was, of all things, one that Taeju knew well. As soon as the owner called him, Taeju got his kids moving and tracked it down. Within four days the thief caught by his crew handed over the bike to Taeju and fled. The problem was, Taeju hadn't returned the bike to the shop owner and continued riding it. A Yamaha R1 could do that to you. The shop owner hadn't turned Taeju in to the cops and seemed to be hoping that the biker would return it on his own.

"Are you sure Taeju has it?" Seungtae asked the snitch.

If they could recover the stolen property before Taeju returned the motorcycle to the owner, the police could get him as an accomplice in burglary.

"I tell you, it's huge!" The snitch even pinpointed where Taeju was staying.

Seungtae said, "Kid, here, that's worth five coupons." In the future, if the snitch was caught for a minor offense, he would be released without any problems, up to five times.

As soon as Seungtae confirmed where Taeju was, he got moving. He had to catch him before Taeju returned the bike or sold it overseas — stolen motorcycles regularly ended up the next day at the port in Pyeongtaek, and the day after, on a cargo ship headed for Cambodia. From a distance Seungtae saw Taeju smoking a cigarette and chatting. Definitely a Yamaha R1. As soon as the kids started moving, Seungtae got on his bike and followed. The gang drove conservatively through the city's evening rush-hour traffic, then made its way down to the Han River walkway. The kids bought instant ramen at a convenience store and hung out some more. Meanwhile, Seungtae called the nearest district police station.

He said, "Come by as if you're doing your usual inspections. They're not wearing helmets so you can get them for that, first.

Since it's a stolen bike, there's a chance they'll run for it. If they do it'll be difficult to catch them, so make sure you have support. The kid with dyed red hair is Oh Taeju — don't let him get away, no matter what. Weapons? I don't think they'll have any. Yeah, I'm here with them, but now isn't the best time to approach them."

The local force did as Seungtae had instructed and the arrest went smoothly. Afterward, Seungtae followed the patrol car. He ate a sandwich at a café near the district station, then walked in while the four bikers were being coerced into making their statements. The kids looked at Seungtae as the traffic officers saluted him.

Seungtae asked, "Who stole it?"

Taeju angrily protested, "But it's not stolen!"

"You're lying, you've got a motorcycle registered as stolen."

"Someone I know had a bike stolen, so I recovered it for them."

"Then why're you riding it? You should've gotten it to its owner . . ."

Taeju hesitated, unable to think of what to say. "I was planning to return it . . ."

"When? Next year? Even not returning money you find on the street is considered embezzlement of lost property."

Taeju frowned and lowered his head.

"Hey, look at me. You don't recognize me?"

"No, I don't."

"Hey, Oh Taeju! You don't recognize me?"

Only then did Taeju begin to guess that the inspection might not be an accident. "Who are you?"

"The pig on the Harley-Davidson. You really don't know who I am?"

Taeju carefully studied Seungtae, then glanced at the Harley parked outside. His suspicions were being confirmed.

Taeju asked, "You didn't come 'cause you got called, did you?"

Seungtae requested that the kids be transferred to the main police headquarters. And Taeju needed to buy time on his home turf and slowly cook up a plan.

28

AS SOON AS SEUNGTAE ENTERED, AS USUAL THE chief of security had something to say. "Still in those clothes?"

Seungtae just scratched his head.

"You still riding that motorcycle all night long?"

"As you ordered the other day, I'm using it only to commute to work and back."

That was a lie. He did everything on it but bust the gangs.

"Is that true?" The chief narrowed his eyes.

Seungtae hesitated but stuck to his story. "There's the issue of jurisdiction, and even if I tail them, there's nothing to gain."

"That's right, that's what I meant. You have nothing to win, so my question is, why get caught up in the whole mess?"

Seungtae simply agreed. "Beats me."

"So you're going to stick to using the bike for commuting?"

"Yes."

"If that's so, it's too bad." The chief of security sat down in the swivel chair. "The situation's changed."

"What situation?"

"You haven't heard yet? One of the traffic officers was chasing down a motorcycle crew and hurt his head when he rolled onto the concrete."

"How bad is it?"

"Not good. Really bad, in fact. He's still unconscious. He's having brain surgery as we speak, but he might as well be dead.

It seems he was holding on to a motorcycle that was getting away and lost his grip."

The chief turned the computer monitor toward Seungtae, showing a photo of the injured officer and his personal information. The chief of security said, "You probably know him."

He was right. Seungtae knew him well. He was a junior colleague of Seungtae's by four years at the previous station where he had worked. He'd had a weakness for alcohol, but he'd been a responsible cop. Seungtae was invited to his wedding but a work emergency came up so he sent congratulatory money instead. It must have been a shotgun wedding; he heard that they had a baby boy soon after.

"I know him well," Seungtae said. "He's got a family too . . ."

"They'll probably hold an official funeral for him. And if he dies, it will be from injuries sustained while on duty. But it's terrible. He was only thirty."

Seungtae rubbed his forehead. "He was a responsible guy."

"An order came from headquarters. Apprehending the criminals responsible for this is a given, as are crackdowns on the motorcycle gangs."

"They have to do something, with one of us ending up like this."

"Headquarters asked for you. Since you were in a magazine, photos and all, they seem to think you're some kind of expert in this area. They're probably going to round up a task force."

"Is this for real?"

"Don't get too excited," said the chief of security. "I said it before, but at most you'll break even when cracking down on these motorcycle crews. The media's talking about how the authority of the government has plummeted — even teens are laughing at the cops. But if we come on too strong, they'll see it as abuse of power or reckless violence."

"So when am I supposed to start?"

"An officer's about to die and you ask when to start? Right away, you'll head to this address first." He slipped a memo to Seungtae. "Now it looks like you can ride that flashy motorcycle all you want."

Seungtae didn't respond.

"And get lots of press."

"First we'll have to find information on the suspect's location."

"How hard can that be? It'll be Independence Movement Day soon, and if you can't stop them before then, it's going to be a real pain." This day commemorated the national uprising on March 1, 1919, against the Japanese colonial government. But for the police, it was a day when hundreds of motorcycles gathered annually for a pain-in-the-ass wild motorcycle run. People called it the Independence Movement Day Grand Motorcycle Rally.

29

LARGE GROUP MOTORCYCLE RUNS HAD EXISTED BE-
fore Jae showed up. The most well known were the Independence Movement Day and Liberation Day motorcycle rallies.
No one knew why the runs happened the night before days related to Japanese colonial rule or who had begun this tradition.
All the police cared about was that the runs had started in the
early 1990s and had continued every year without fail.

No one welcomed the tradition except the motorcycle crews.
They weren't being secretly funded, and no one offered them
any moral support either. Even the intellectuals who yearned
for a world governed by "the people" didn't think of the bikers
as "the people." And the nationalists who despised the Japanese
disapproved of the young troublemakers.

The runs didn't descend into full-blown violence — like ri-
oting or arson, or murder or rape. They did sometimes threaten
other drivers who complained, and they heckled pedestrians,
but they rarely caused any real damage. The kids just raced all
night long, and like guerrilla fighters, played hide-and-seek, trying to elude the sluggish police. They didn't have a political aim
or a slogan. They wanted something extremely simple. A midnight parade, that was all.

At one point the police debated legalizing the runs. They
thought that the motorcycle gang's leader could report upcom-

ing rallies, and with a police escort, the bikers would be permitted to gather within a restricted area of the city and race as much as they wanted.

Even the chief commissioner of the National Police Agency supported this proposal before it came to a dead end. The problem was, no one could find this reputed leader.

At the task force meeting, Seungtae said, "Actually, they kind of have a leader." He pulled up his PowerPoint slides.

"Have a look at this graph," he said. "A group of kids called the front guard go out first and block the intersection so no other cars can pass. It's similar to when our cars control traffic when we're guarding a VIP. Then their leader shows up, usually swinging a light wand in the air, and heads the parade. The front guard controls traffic until the entire group passes, and then follows them from the back. So they become the rear guard. The leader gets instant updates on police movements while leading a large run, and makes decisions based on what he hears. That means he's got to have a deep understanding of the city's layout, not to mention leadership skills and courage."

"So all we need to do is get this leader or boss, whatever they call it."

Seungtae nodded at Senior Police Officer Pyo Seokwon. "The problem is, this leader's incredibly hard to arrest at the actual site. Our patrol cars have to press through the front guard, push all the riders into the center of the road, and then start hunting for the leader within the group. He'll be the one who rides the best. They're about two to three times faster than us — and fearless. They act like it's no big deal if they die. Didn't they put one of our cops into a coma? And the motorcycle run he was after wasn't even a big one."

"It doesn't look easy."

"Another thing — the leader often changes. Whoever's the craziest at the moment ends up being boss. For example, if Rider A leading the group isn't riding too well, Rider B will show up and push him out. If Rider A's pushed aside, he'll retreat to the back without complaint. They're like male lions in the animal kingdom. They don't claw and fight each other to death. It's 'So you're a better rider than me? Then you be boss,' and Rider A will back off."

"Then they're not an actual group?"

"That's right," said Seungtae. "If they were a real group, we would squeeze from the top and catch them one after the other, but these guys aren't like that. Meaning, they're not real gangs. They're more like a mob, and that makes them hard to bust."

"So even if we did catch their leader, it's no use because they won't follow his orders. If they had a police-escorted parade, or were told they can ride on the Yongin motor racetrack, no one would show up."

Seungtae carefully studied the other officers on the task force. If they didn't understand the mindset of the motorcycle gangs now, they never would. Seungtae was used to the state of being physically present but mentally elsewhere. He was skillful enough to hide it, but still it disturbed him like a continual ringing in the ear. At least psychologically, he still had more in common with the motorcycle gangs. Riding motorcycles inspired bonding and kinship. Even if he rode a Harley-Davidson and the kids rode 125cc bikes that were made in China, they were the same people — they all risked their lives to fly through the air. Those tucked in automobiles protected by seat belts and airbags couldn't understand what this meant.

Seungtae continued. "That's right. No one would come because the kids don't just want to ride — they want to ride dangerously. Why do you think they don't wear helmets? They'd lose street cred!"

"What if the police stop busting them? Wouldn't they quit after it stopped being fun?"

Officer Pyo said, "The press would print headlines like LAW-LESSNESS IN THE CITY: WHERE ARE THE POLICE?"

Everyone laughed politely.

Seungtae agreed. "You're right, the kids are the leads and we're the supporting actors. If we weren't around, the kids would definitely get bored and stop. But we have to be present. The kids know we have no choice but to show up. When they start a big run, they assume we'll come. If we pursue them, they escape, and it happens again and again. The only ones who suffer are the young drafted police doing their military service."

Captain Lee, who had the highest rank on the task force — a supervisor for them all, in a way — sat silently in the corner and chuckled. "Sounds fun. I'd like to ride in a big motorcycle run too."

He added, "So can't we keep pace with them and just make sure there are no accidents? They'll be the ones slammed in the press. We can pick up a reasonable number of them and turn them in right away for traffic violations, and the press can jot down the stats."

Seungtae pushed back. "That's what we've done till now, but the situation's changed, as you all know."

Officer Pyo muttered, "Can we tie them to a fake gang?"

Captain Lee smiled mysteriously and stood up. "Who knows? There could be an organization behind them. All you have to do is draw the right picture."

The first meeting ended. It was windy when Seungtae stepped outside. As soon as the young drafted officers drinking coffee and smoking saw Seungtae, they retreated. Distraught people hovered with their cell phones in front of the patrol office, and police returning from the field came in one by one.

Seungtae had once briefly worked at the Seoul main office. The endless paperwork bored him and the building's stale air suffocated him. What he disliked most was that the only people around him were police officers; he'd been no different from any other public servant. An officer fully knows his identity only by encountering the public. When Seungtae was first appointed, the chief of police said to him, "A police officer is the nation, and the phrase 'police nation' is a tautology. The nation is the police. We have a monopoly on violence, and with that violence we run the nation."

No matter how complex the case, a well-trained judicial police officer had to be able to make a one-sentence report. Whether a person had murdered hundreds over decades, or set fire to Namdaemun Gate, Honginmun Gate, and the National Museum of Korea, the report boiled down to that one sentence. When Seungtae first learned how to write these reports at the police academy, no one taught him why a single sentence was important, but now he understood. The one lucid sentence actually told the person under investigation this:

We have no interest in hearing every word of your story or

"why you had to do it." The mess you made can be — and has to be — summarized in one sentence.

Even the police statements were steeped in the mentality of having a legal monopoly on violence. Though the totality of this violence increasingly made Seungtae uncomfortable, he couldn't pinpoint why. Ironically, he finally and suddenly understood when he was surrounded by protesters at a violent demonstration. Even after the mayhem dissolves and everyone returns home, the police are still there. They might act remorseful for the public, but they don't actually give in. That's the nature of the force. At a demonstration rife with lampoonery and mockery, it's easy to ridicule the police weighed down in riot gear. The police — the nation — is slow but it is also stubborn. It doesn't forget. By using its collected photos and evidence, it slowly makes you realize who is the ultimate source of violence. So the police force is less like a vampire and more like a zombie. It doesn't pay attention to what others think. It doesn't need attention, and doesn't rely on its charisma. Instead it creeps along tenaciously in pursuit of its goal. And when it goes in for the kill, it jumps in and breaks every bone.

Seungtae knew deep down that a part of him rejected this police mindset. He wanted his charisma to move others to action. But the magic was destroyed as soon as people knew he was a cop. He would brandish all his official power at them, as if getting revenge, then later feel disgusted with himself.

It happened exactly this way when he got Taeju. This kid was more disgusted by than afraid of Seungtae, as if he wasn't even worth hating. He wasn't even interested in Seungtae's Harley. He was only interested in returning as quickly as possible to his friends and his girl. One day Seungtae took Taeju out of the station.

"You don't want to go to reform school, do you?" asked Seungtae. "Well, it all depends on you."

He took Taeju to his apartment and, just as his camp teacher had done to him long ago, he handcuffed Taeju from the back and pushed him down. Violence under the guise of legalized violence. Afterward, he gave him coupons — like the ones he'd given his spies. Taeju's protests had been more muted than he'd expected.

Seungtae said, "I'll get the theft charge cleared, don't worry."

They headed to a bar and ordered fried chicken. When the owner said he couldn't serve alcohol to minors, Seungtae pulled out his badge. Taeju silently drank his beer and gnawed at a drumstick. Then Seungtae received a text message.

A police officer had confirmed the identity of a motorcycle gang member wanted in connection to the death of the police officer. Now all they had to focus on was Independence Movement Day. Seungtae put away his cell phone and asked Taeju, "Any chance you've heard about a guy named Jae?"

Taeju frowned and avoided Seungtae's eyes. He stayed silent.

"Asshole, you think what a grownup says means nothing? You know him, or not?"

Taeju gazed blankly at him. That look stirred up the shame

buried deep inside Seungtae. He bounded up and twisted Tae-ju's arms behind his back, which shocked the other customers. Seungtae handcuffed him, and Taeju smirked.

"You're laughing at me? You asshole, what . . ."

Taeju spit in Seungtae's face and kicked the chairs over. As the bar erupted in anarchy, the bar owner motioned to call the police.

Seungtae yelled, "Hey, I said I'm a cop!"

The bar owner ignored him and dialed 112. Within minutes, a patrol car arrived. Once the uniformed officer saw the hand-cuffs on Taeju and Seungtae's badge, he asked what had happened.

"I was arresting a wanted criminal. Let me finish up here," he said, speaking informally to show how relaxed he was. But the cop didn't back off and looked doubtful as he took in the scene. The cop said, "Since it was a 112 call, we have to file a report."

"Write it the way it happened, that Lieutenant Pak Seungtae had to use force while arresting a wanted man."

When Seungtae was dragging Taeju out, the bar owner blocked the way. "Sir, the bill . . ."

Seungtae's face heated up. Taeju cackled mightily, and the departing officer left without saluting Seungtae. Only after he shook off the others did Seungtae swipe the spit off his face.

He said to Taeju, "You asshole. You're a goner."

30

AM I EVIL? SEUNGTAE LOOKED DOWN AT TAEJU — AT his bruised body, handcuffed and collapsed on its side — and stroked his own chest. Seungtae was well built and sculpted by exercise. He was young and fit, and could be with anyone he wanted. So why did it always end with him and a boy? He had been in a number of serious relationships, but he was always left feeling hollow. This emptiness subsided only when his darkest side emerged.

Then Taeju said, "Shit, give me some water. And do something about these handcuffs."

Seungtae unlocked the cuffs and brought water back from the kitchen. Taeju gulped it down.

"How are you?" Seungtae asked.

Taeju squinted as if guessing his intent.

"Are you okay?"

Taeju rubbed at his hurt wrist instead of answering.

"If you ever get caught running a light or something, call me. A burglary or attack is tougher."

"Can I leave now?"

"You still haven't answered my question."

"What was it?"

"About that guy, Jae."

"Do you know Mokran? The girl who rides a Kawasaki. She's kind of famous . . . She's my ex."

Seungtae wasn't really interested in the girls. "I don't know her."

"She's dating him, I guess. His crew's on fire these days."

"More than yours?"

"They're smaller in number, but different. You should meet him sometime." The corners of his lips lifted meaningfully.

"Different? In what way?"

"The fucker's different. Just one look and you know. Can I go now?"

"Yeah. Next time you get a text from this big brother, don't ignore it. I'll get you for that."

Just before he stepped out of the doorway, Taeju bowed and said, "Thank you for the fucked-up experience. Drive carefully when you're out at night, you perv."

He banged the door shut and stomped down the stairs. Seungtae didn't follow him. He grinned to himself. If Taeju acted like this, there would be no loose ends later. Boys like Taeju had mixed feelings about yielding to violence. They couldn't separate accepting it as the defeated one, and morally rejecting it. He saw this in the most pathetic ones, who believed if they lost to someone stronger, they had to accept the consequences. It wasn't that they didn't want revenge, but they didn't think they had the right to complain. This was probably why the sexual abuse of boys stayed hidden for so long, or even remained buried forever.

At the balcony, Seungtae saw the late spring snow falling outside. He slid open the glass door, extended his arm toward the chilly snowflakes.

31

THOUGH IT WASN'T INDEPENDENCE MOVEMENT DAY

yet, flags were everywhere, hanging lifelessly as if spent from the heat. Seungtae climbed into Officer Pyo's modest Hyundai Accent. When Seungtae had said he would take his Harley there, the captain, unofficial head of the task force, said, "If you come rumbling up, you think the kids will stay put and say, 'Please, come get me'?"

Seungtae was already well known among the motorcycle crews, who called him "the Harley cop." Since he'd only fine the kids for misdemeanors, they hadn't been so guarded around him. Some were even pleased to see him. They viewed him as someone who understood biking culture and "at least speaks our language." But the past few months had changed that. Articles criticizing the motorcycle gangs popped up daily. The officer in a coma died, his organs donated. This didn't stop the gangs from racing every weekend, so the papers attacked the authorities as incompetent and the online comments criticized the gangs: send them to the slammer or to military service, get them with a net, use guns on them; even send them to North Korea. The motorcycle gangs were one of the few groups that the entire public could loathe together. In the day, people complained if their Chinese food was delivered a few minutes late, and at night, they cursed the bikers for ignoring the laws and creating chaos.

Seungtae often used his spies to arrest the kids during motorcycle rallies, but public opinion was so low that the sacrifice of a few victims wouldn't be enough. The higher-ups in the federal court and the police force wanted to hand over real numbers to the press. No one cared what happened to the kids post-arrest. As crackdowns continued, the gangs began keeping their distance from Seungtae; it had been a long time since they had eaten instant ramen together and swapped jokes. The climax of it all would be Independence Movement Day.

That day Jae's name became famous in the biking world. Taeju was in Seungtae's grip and relatively tame on the bike, but Jae's group came storming out. The police defense line around the Mapo and Yongsan districts collapsed. The riding that had started at midnight kept on until dawn; callers flooded the 112 emergency hotline with complaints.

Seungtae had first seen Jae the night before Independence Movement Day. Seungtae had been driving the Accent, disguised as one of the cars that followed the motorcycle rallies. He cut into their ranks, but he didn't make it to the front, so at first he failed to catch sight of Jae. But as soon as he radioed in and ordered patrol cars to block the group, Jae reversed direction. The leader's yellow baton and long hair were an immediate tip-off.

"That one must be Jae," Seungtae muttered.

As Taeju promised, he had recognized him right away.

He could tell Jae was tall even on his motorcycle, and with his hair flying behind him he looked like a general on a horse. He skillfully handled the 125cc Honda one-handed and his gaze swept over the area. Officer Pyo took dozens of photos with a zoom lens, but it was too dark and the riders were moving quickly; the images looked like blurry phantoms. Still, Jae made a deep impression on Seungtae. He knew that if they met again, he would immediately recognize the kid. As Taeju had promised, Jae was different from the others. He seemed to float calmly in the saddle. His emaciated body, tattered coat, and messy hair suited the motorcycle, and his way of leading the group was cool-headed and intelligent.

"So the celebrity's shown up on a bike," said Officer Pyo. "The little piece of shit."

Seungtae regretted not pursuing and busting Jae earlier. Messages from his spies continued coming in. "They say he showed up in the Seodaemun district last night" and "Jae's said to have wiped out the whole Wangsimni neighborhood."

When tip-offs arrived in the morning, the information was useless — too late and lacking credibility. It was hard not to laugh at a report from a second-generation CEO's kid rebelling by riding with motorcycle crews. In any case when Seungtae added up the information, it looked like Jae didn't have an official job anywhere, so it wasn't going to be easy to find him. And even if Seungtae did, what could he pin on him? He had no choice but to catch Jae red-handed.

Seungtae had searched online forums for a few days, but he didn't find much. A forum would pop up right before a motorcycle rally but get taken down just after, and most were written in indecipherable slang and code. His spies said that the most essential information, such as time and place, was communicated by text on the day of the rally.

He made little progress in tracking down Jae before Liberation Day, August 15, until trouble broke out at an unexpected location. Around the end of June, local police from Suwon had hauled in a gang of teenagers who had been fighting. The few officers present in the cramped local station struggled to subdue the two groups, who were punching each other. Once peace was established and the kids were called in and threatened into writing reports, the police heard an uproar outside. They stepped out, assuming they'd find a car accident, then fled back, but it was too late. Some motorcycle gang members carrying lumber and steel pipes forced their way into the station. While the frightened police scrambled to get away, the perpetrators escaped on their bikes, along with the original group in custody.

The next day the press printed articles with headlines like TEENAGERS SCORN AUTHORITY ALL THE WAY UP TO THE LOCAL POLICE STATION, borrowing from movies with titles such as *Assault on Precinct 13*. Based on information they had already collected on the gang's whereabouts, the police managed to round up some of the aggressors.

All of them said the same thing: "Talk to Jae."

Seungtae examined a security camera file of the attack collected through the police computer network. It was definitely Jae from Independence Movement Day. He hadn't entered the station, but had silently watched as his guys created havoc, and casually slipped away as soon as the assault ended.

Watching the screen, Pyo remarked, "We could probably get him on a preliminary warrant."

"But we don't know where he is right now."

"That's true."

"Now we can even get him for obstructing official duty, down to committing violent crime."

"Not we *can* get him, but we *will* get him. I mean, he's a total psychopath. They're not an activist group demonstrating, like in '88. They had the nerve to hit up a police station."

It was simple math that taught them that the group was usually active in Suwon, so more resources were allocated to the satellite city after the attack. It looked as if they would catch their target. But the case wasn't wrapped up as easily as Seungtae had expected. First, Jae himself was difficult to track down. No one knew where he'd turn up, outside of the large motorcycle rallies. The fact that he had even appeared in Suwon meant that he could be anywhere on the outskirts of Seoul — from Euijeongbu to Ilsan. Worse, after the attack, Jae became a legend. Rumors that he had planned the police station raid spread like wildfire within motorcycle circles. Jae had first started gaining a reputation on Independence Movement Day, and now essentially acquired a brilliant halo.

Still, each kid they caught said the same thing about Jae: "I said I don't know! Everyone just calls him Jae."

They raided Jae's former sleeping quarters (discovered through the kids' tip-offs), but they only managed to terrify a bunch of sleeping girls and boys.

Officer Pyo, who'd listened to Seungtae's complaints, said

casually, "Maybe the asshole's a spy." How about sending a notice out on the police intranet system? Who knows? Someone could have once put him in reform school or something. It's not like we have to prove ourselves by catching him, as long as we stop the big rally on Liberation Day."

Few organizations guard their information or are as uncooperative with each other as the police. It's common for police station A to pursue a criminal, and for station B to catch and release him, so when Captain Lee said that he would summarize the file they had on Jae and upload it onto the intranet system, Seungtae didn't expect much. But soon enough someone called Seungtae's office phone.

A man said, "I know a little about this Jae kid."

From his tone, Seungtae guessed that the man was an old hand in their field. Seungtae said, "Would you mind telling me which division you're from?"

After telling Seungtae which station he was based at, and his position, he said, "Sir, I'll come to you."

Seungtae added politely, "No, I've got business around Seoul Station. Will you be in this afternoon?"

32

OFFICER PYO STIRRED IN HIS SEAT. "WILL WE HAVE
a helicopter today? They said no, didn't they?"

It was a sweltering day and the sewers stank.

Seungtae sighed. "The answer's no. They just don't get it.
No matter how many times you tell them you can't follow the
rally's path without a helicopter, guys at headquarters smirk and
say, 'You want to send a helicopter late at night chasing after a
bunch of bitches on motorcycles? You think this is Los Ange-
les?' Assholes."

Seungtae had guessed they'd respond that way. But today's
motorcycle rally was different from previous ones. You got an
idea of how big it would be from watching the numbers rise and
fall on the rally's online forums. Even Seungtae's spies seemed
excited. Like soccer fans anticipating the World Cup every four
years, the motorcycle gangs eagerly awaited the rally. The difference was that no one knew when a "genuine" gigantic motorcycle rally would happen. But word was quickly spreading that
the upcoming Liberation Day might be the big day that all the
gangs had been waiting for.

"How many do you think will show up?" Pyo fiddled with a
camera.

"How many do you think?" Seungtae asked back.

"I'm guessing around five hundred?" Pyo looked as if he
might have overshot.

"Multiply that by ten."

"Five thousand? Hey, that's taking it too far."

"Just watch. You'll know why I said we absolutely need a helicopter."

What would five thousand motorcycles sound like? Seungtae had never seen such a sight. And what if the motorcycles were customized to be even more deafening during the rally? The thought excited him as someone who rode a bike, even if he had to maneuver through them to arrest the leader and disband the ranks. The motorcycle was inferior to the automobile — no matter how classy your bike, it was a second-class citizen on the road. You could say that the only time this order was reversed was during a major motorcycle rally, but each time it was Seungtae's fate to be opposing it. As soon as he thought this, he could hardly bear the stocky detectives' stifling Hyundai Accent. Their breath smelled of cigarettes and spicy beef soup; and the air conditioner couldn't handle the midsummer heat, the four men's body heat, and the boiling asphalt.

Seungtae grabbed his walkie-talkie and checked on the progress. It was nine in the evening and there was no sign of movement yet. In the alleys he saw kids smoking by their motorcycles, and though he knew what they were waiting for, he couldn't do anything about it — not yet. He felt his powerlessness, and for him this emotion inevitably grew into self-hatred. He struggled to escape the sordid muddiness of his feelings. Only violence could expel the inner darkness.

Seungtae reassured everyone. "It's going to be an incredible night."

He rolled down the window and let in the humid heat, which flicked across his cheek like a cow's tongue.

"I can't take it anymore," he said, and lurched out of the car. "I'll go on my own. It's too suffocating in here."

"You sure?"

"Yeah, I'll get my Harley from the station."

Pyo, annoyed that the cool air was seeping from the car, slammed the door shut.

33

AUGUST 14, 10 P.M. TRAFFIC HAD THINNED, AND
downtown Seoul was quiet, but moving. Most traffic cops, even
those who were off duty, had been mobilized. After they set up
barricades at checkpoints on the Han River's bridges, they began inspections. The crews that came on the state roads from
the cities of Suwon, Anyang, Uijongbu, Gunpo, Uiwang, Pyeongtaek, Yangpyeong, and Paju were on standby in Yongsan,
Mapo, Gangnam, Seocho, Guro, Ttukseom, and Wangsimni.
There was no sign of the press; they made a fuss only after a motorcycle rally ended. Though they knew the rally was an annual
event, the media didn't assign reporters to cover it and instead
sent them to police headquarters the next morning for a briefing
— and then they wrote up short articles. The night before Liberation Day, a few junior reporters chose to write about the tense
preparations as well as about their buddies in the force, but that
was voluntary.

If as many as fifty students or citizens gathered, cameras
crowded in. These people stayed in the same spot — their main
interest to get the attention of the middle class — and they were
photogenic with their picket signs, and candles. They chanted
slogans together. In contrast, the motorcycle crews were hard to
keep up with. It wasn't easy to take a shot of a motorcycle racing by late at night, since the photographer had to also sit pre-

cariously on a motorcycle and somehow take photos with the appropriate exposure and shutter speed. The night before Liberation Day, the motorcycle crews and the police felt the tension building, but the general public had no clue about what was going on.

Seungtae was at a gas station, waiting for a green light, when heavy engine sounds from behind startled him. Over a hundred deluxe motorcycles were slowing down at a pelican crossing. Their riders were over forty years old and wore expensive leather jackets, boots, and knee guards. Seungtae was familiar with this kind of motorcycle club, which usually assembled on weekend mornings and went for drives nearby to Yangpyeong or Chunaju. They rarely gathered at night, generally stayed in one lane, obeyed traffic lights, and were careful drivers.

Their engines revved up as soon as the light turned green. Seungtae kept up with them as he rode, his Harley blending in with theirs. Though he knew where they were headed, he followed quietly. They passed the Gongdeok neighborhood, where the *Hankyoreh* newspaper building stood on a hill, then raced toward Seoul Station. The police waiting at the roadside didn't attempt to restrain them, and some of them even waved. The bikers stopped in front of the War Memorial Museum in the Yongsan district and parked. Some smoked, others got instant coffee from a vending machine. Seungtae recognized a few of them when they took off their helmets.

"So we meet here," he said as he approached a young dermatologist who worked in the Apkujeong neighborhood.

"Ah, Lieutenant Pak, when did you arrive? I didn't see you when we took off."

"Yes, well . . . that . . ."

"This is the life, riding in the city at night. How have you been these days?"

"You know, the same as always," he replied.

The leader soon approached the group, carrying coffee and talking on his cell phone. When he saw Seungtae, the businessman who owned a golf gear store near Nambu Bus Terminal looked pleased. He slipped the cell phone into his pocket and said, "You came! We were just going to handle it on our own."

"I happened to be passing by and . . ."

"Sure, just passing by." The leader continued. "The text I got a while back said we're going to start around midnight. We'll head over as soon as we get the location. We'll stick close to them from the back, then cut through them like bamboo, force our way into the center of the rally, and divide them in half. Those shits'll be freaked out just hearing our engines from behind."

He added that the police had to consider human rights and all that, so their speed and mobility suffered and they couldn't get to the rallies on time. If they didn't do it, it just wouldn't happen. This time they had to correct the kids' bad habits once and for all.

The other club members were nearly frothing at the mouth. Seungtae had always known that they were the teenage motorcycle gangs' greatest enemies. To them, the gangs were evil — they habitually ruined any clean-cut image of biking culture. For years these older bikers had lobbied for touring motorcycles with greater horsepower to legally ride on highways — common in Europe and the United States — but they hadn't gotten it past the front door of the National Assembly precisely because of the motorcycle gangs. National Assembly members didn't even consider passing the bill because the press on bikers was so bad.

If you wanted to change the law, you had to make that change possible.

The motorcycle club members understood the media message. These overeducated Jekylls started riding motorcycles precisely because it was dangerous, but now they had to prove their law-abiding spirit and awareness of safety. To do that, they had to kill the Hyde dormant within them. Most of these middle-aged fans of motorcycles converted because they hated the comfort of the automobile. They set themselves apart by treating their peers as snobs who sank into plush leather car seats and valued their seat belts and airbags. When these bikers wrapped bandanas around their heads and went for a drive in the suburbs, they looked down at those in cars. For they believed themselves to be real men, wild at heart. Their nagging wives, saying, *You've got to stop, it's too dangerous!* only boosted their macho pride. Their narcissism was as solid as a wall until they encountered a bunch of helmetless teenagers in cheap slippers zooming through the city. So they became enraged each time the motorcycle gangs made headlines because the gangs' very existence made these older bikers look like the conservative snobs. One could say they had assembled the night before Liberation Day in order to restore their image. But now, faced with a massive motorcycle rally, they were as excited as the teenage crews. Behind the pretense of guiding the teenagers and establishing a healthy motorcycling culture, they were actually thrilled to use their "babies" as weapons while the police looked the other way.

34

THE LIBERATION DAY MOTORCYCLE RALLY BEGAN

just before midnight. Jae texted everyone the meeting point, which was the symbolically important Gwanghwamun district, the center of government. Groups from neighborhoods such as Noryangjin, Bulgwangdong, Ttukseom, Gurodong, Sangamdong, Sangbongdong, and Wangsimni headed for Gwanghwamun. The gathering was already enormous. People could see the bikes leaping out recklessly from alleys left and right and merging throughout the city. Jae's crew, which had started out east from Noryangjin, ran into another crew of twenty around the Dongjakdong neighborhood.

"Where you coming from?" asked Gas Tank, who was riding in front. He got his nickname because he delivered canisters of LP gas from house to house.

"From Seosan!" someone yelled.

"From where?"

"Seosan in Chungcheon province. You don't know Seosan?"

Jae's crew sped toward Banpo Bridge, following the group from Seosan, who had left there at nine-thirty. The front guard went first and blocked traffic at the intersections so Jae's crew could race ahead without stopping for lights.

Some crew members in their twenties, who had completed their military service as drafted police, headed straight for the traffic panel box at intersections and manipulated the lights.

At every few intersections they ran into patrol officers, but they ignored them. The sight of the fatigued officers only boosted their morale. A succession of modified bikes darted out and followed them. It was clear they hadn't just been out riding and by chance joined the rally. They kept hollering from bikes dressed up with gadgets and flashing LED lights. It was a festival that some had anticipated for a long time, a parade.

That night Mokran showed up on her Kawasaki. She maintained a steady interval between her and Jae throughout the rally, and I kept them in sight as I rode behind. Since new bikers who didn't understand our planned signals kept squeezing in, the rally began more slowly than normal.

"How many you think'll show up today?" asked Seesaw Eyes, who was riding right up against my bike. He was an old friend of Gas Tank and had run with Jae's crew for a long time.

Gas Tank predicted, "From the look of it, maybe a thousand?"

Seesaw Eyes said, "Hell, I'm practically shitting myself."

Jae sent Seesaw Eyes, who was too excited to stay back, to cover the front. Jae kept watch on the rally behind him while posting guys at each intersection. When Seesaw Eyes parked his bike and kicked the rearview mirror off a honking Audi, the driver got scared and cowered in the car.

When the crew received several reports that police barricades had nearly blocked off Gwanghwamun, Jae immediately changed the meeting point to the Jongmyo entrance. The number of text messages exploded. As Jae crossed Banpo Bridge, a gust of wind blew off the yellow flag that had been hanging on his bike. For the first time since leaving Noryangjin, the rally halted. Someone sprinted out and grabbed the flag, which had caught on a rail, and fastened it firmly back in place. No one considered this ominous. They were all still too young to believe in omens. The line of bikes started moving again. The police at each checkpoint tried to move the physical barricade farther down, but they couldn't shut down heavily trafficked bridges yet. The sound of thousands of motorcycles spitting out exhaust could be heard from two kilometers away — like bees buzzing in their hive.

The other bikers cleared a path as soon as Jae's motorcycle appeared. Those of us who'd followed Jae continued racing after him. It took over twenty minutes for the thousands of bikes gathered at Jongmyo to depart. The guys' shouts and the girls' shrieks blended with the roaring engines and blaring horns. Around the Jongno area, cars waited to join the rally — the so-called car-*pok* on standby. As if escorting the motorcycles, they lined up to the left and, with their emergency lights on, moved forward. Tow trucks, delivery trucks, and compact cars driven by former motorcycle-crew members stuck close to the bikes.

People returning home late watched the bikers with exhaustion and awe. A major motorcycle rally was no different from a typhoon — you heard rumors of its approach everywhere. Everyone began anticipating it, but no one knew exactly when and how it would hit. If you were lucky, you would steer clear of it without trouble. And even if you ran directly into it, it was difficult to grasp its full scope.

The front guard now operated intuitively. Without receiving orders to do so, the front and rear guards took turns blocking the flow of traffic. There were a few patrol cars present, but they were kept back so far away by the sheer mass of bikes that they could only look on. Motorcycle crews now controlled the city. Frightened people who didn't dare catch a taxi watched the members with loathing, and cab drivers losing business during their busiest hour shouted curses like "I hope your head breaks open and you spend your life a vegetable, asshole!"

The massive rally continued throughout the city's main streets. Alarmed when woken by the roar, many people called 112. Then around one in the morning, the police force shifted tactics. The barricades started to come down, and the traffic officers began to round up the front guard.

We ran into the motorcycle club near Mapo Police Station. They showed up at the back of the motorcycle rally. At first we assumed they were just another bike crew joining in, so we immediately made room for them, but we quickly realized that they weren't following the leader's orders or the unspoken rules of the rally. These heavyweight, high-horsepower motorcycles forced their way to the lead, where Jae was. The riders couldn't have been more different from us, with their black leather clothes and their bikes done up in bright colors. As soon as someone in the crowd shouted, "The assholes are cops!" our line of motorcycles scattered. Some approached the motorcycle club while brandishing iron pipes. When a weak 100cc bike suddenly wedged itself between the large motorcycles, a BMW and a Harley-Davidson wobbled and flipped onto the pavement. The other club members got scared and tried to retreat, but it was hard to escape the stream of oncoming bikes.

Jae saw the chaotic scene behind him as he rode over a hill. Sensing that something was wrong, he slowed down and returned to the rear. He shouted, "What is it? What's the problem?"

Someone shouted at Jae, "Fuck, it's the cops."

"Shake them off," he said.

Just then, a Harley-Davidson went full throttle toward Jae. The guy riding it said, "Hey, you're Jae, right?"

Jae looked in the Harley's direction. "Who're you?"

"You don't know me? The Harley cop. Lieutenant Pak Seung-tae. I'm Lieutenant Pak. You don't know who I am?"

The rear of the motorcycle ranks was becoming increasingly disorganized. The front seemed to be facing trouble too, and the rally was losing speed.

"Who?" asked Jae.

The thunderous sound of motorcycle engines and horns made talking impossible, but Seungtae continued shouting. The only thing Jae heard over the noise was "cop." The crew members near Jae surrounded Seungtae. Mokran and I were a little ahead of Jae. When I looked back, Gas Tank had come up from behind Seungtae's Harley and was kicking the bike's tail with his foot. Jae accelerated and escaped ahead. Some bikers were aiming their iron pipes at Seungtae's back and head, but his Harley rode low and wasn't easy to overturn. He slowed down and dodged their attacks.

Jae headed south; we had stirred up the downtown area as much as possible. He picked Gangnam as the next destination since law enforcement had been lax there, so far. But the police response was escalating; the patrol officers formed a line and pushed the rear guard aside. They began cutting off the rally's tail.

35

AFTER JAE'S MASSIVE RALLY PASSED THROUGH THE
area, the only people remaining were motorcycle club members. Their attack on the run had failed, and some of them had
damaged their motorcycles. Ambulances raced in and carted off
the injured. Seungtae parked his overheated Harley, squatted on
the pavement, and watched the roaring mass move farther away.
His lower back throbbed from the pummeling he'd received.

The dermatologist's BMW stopped near him, and he asked
Seungtae, "What are you doing? Did you get hurt?"

"No, I'm fine."

He got out of the car and offered Seungtae a cigarette.

"I don't smoke."

"They're a bit frightening, seeing them close-up like that."

"It's because they're fearless. How do you win with guys who
aren't scared of dying?"

Seungtae had also been afraid. When the pipe had come
down on his back and head, he'd been helpless. Thankfully,
the kids had been steering their bikes while attacking, so the
hits were softened. Still, if he hadn't instinctively lifted his arm
and blocked them, he might now be rolling on the pavement.
Within the police force, Seungtae held the most moderate views
on the bikers. He had opposed cracking down on them because
he knew too well that catching hundreds, no, thousands of them

wouldn't stop them. His theory was that the largest crews would slowly shrink in number with guidance and preemptive crackdowns, and after that, controlling them with traffic laws would be sufficient. Above all, Seungtae knew that they weren't the scum they were made out to be on the Internet. When you actually met them, they really were just kids. Innocent and easily frightened. If they received a text that scared them before a large rally, many didn't even show up.

But Jae was different. Normally when Seungtae approached a boy, even if he was a leader, he would shrink back. He would be intimidated just by the fact that a police officer knew his name. But Jae's crew had actually attacked Seungtae, and they had shrugged off an attack by heavyweight motorcycles.

This kid was dangerous.

Over the past few months, Seungtae had collected more information on Jae. He now knew where Jae was born, how he had grown up, and his current living situation. Seungtae had spoken to the director of the orphanage and received relevant documents, and had even more paperwork concerning Jae piled up on his desk. He'd recently acquired evidence suggesting that Jae wasn't just a rebellious kid but someone with ambitions toward political and spiritual leadership, like Malcolm X.

It was no easy task leading thousands of motorcycles across the city. You needed an animal's instinct and an intimacy with the city's roads and sudden curves, and, on top of all this, you needed to anticipate police action. Jae managed to accomplish all of this with basic methods like flag and hand signals and text messages.

Seeing Jae close up, it was hard to continue thinking of him as a teenager. Even Seungtae, who had encountered countless numbers of gangs, felt awe the moment he approached Jae and the yellow flag attached to his pitiful 125cc bike. The baptism of steel pipes that had flown at Seungtae directly afterward felt like the punishment he deserved for being disrespectful. Of course that feeling faded as soon as he left the rally. It was like waking up from a spell. An unbearable emptiness replaced admiration; it was like an emotional hangover.

"Block them at the Han River, you bitches!" Shouts from the National Police Agency situation room nearly burned out Seungtae's walkie-talkie. Commissioners with ranks and names he didn't know were yelling at him while watching the CCTV images transmitted on screen.

"If they reach Gangnam, just wait and see what happens to all of you!"

His superiors kept repeating that the motorcycle rally must be stopped, clueless about its size. It was three or four times bigger than any motorcycle rally Seungtae had known. Even if you cut off its tail, the riders merely took detours then rejoined the main body. Jae had kept security tight up to the rally, and then once it began, lithely crossed the city, which he seemed able to read. It was enough to make you suspect that someone was helping him by watching the road conditions from a control room.

Seungtae drove down to the Itaewon neighborhood where a task force was on standby. Itaewon was a strategic area in Seoul where foreign forces were stationed. The Qing military had based itself there during the Sino-Japanese War, and after the Korean War, the American army did so as well. From here, you had a bird's-eye view of the Han River, with easy access to both north and south.

As soon as Seungtae joined the Special Response Team, he sent a text message: "Which bridge will they cross? That's all I need to know."

A response came promptly back: "Hannam."

He asked Pyo, "Where are the kids right now?"

"They're in Daehangno."

"Then we've got less than ten minutes. It'll be Hannam Bridge. Tell them to set up a barricade. Divert the traffic, and block Banpo Bridge. Dongho Bridge too."

The task force members drove to Hannam Bridge. One squadron of the conscripted police force had already arrived on the scene.

Seungtae hustled to the front. "In groups of two, attack with batons. Go at them from both sides. They'll slow down around this point, so don't be scared to just pull them down. There'll be a bike with a yellow flag attached to it — don't let that guy get away. He's a wanted man. He'll be up front. Catching him is your goal. Whoever brings him in gets a bonus vacation, commissioner's orders."

36

JAE TOOK THE LEAD AS THEY HEADED TOWARD HAN-
nam Bridge. The traffic officers waiting near Namsan Tunnel
Two aggressively cut the rally off in the middle. Because they
attacked from the front, they nearly ran into Jae's bike. But
Jae avoided the patrol cars with his dazzling maneuvers, then
emerged up front again. He looked back at the patrol cars. About
a third of the bikers had been marooned by the police, but Jae
didn't stop. He continued toward Hannam Bridge. He probably thought the cut-off group could join again later. He stopped
the ranks of bikes still behind him on the Hannam Bridge over-
pass.

"What is it?" Mokran asked me.

"Look at that. There are cops all across the bridge. It looks
like Jae's trying to turn the group around."

"But some are already crossing." Mokran said, pointing at
the Oksu neighborhood. The motorcycles cut off by the police
were now detouring toward Oksu. It was clear that they would
make it south to Gangnam by crossing the Dongho Bridge. As
if Jae had made his decision, he signaled to those behind him
with a wave of his flashing baton, meaning, *Go at top speed and
break through*. For if they backed off now, the only ones remembered would be the group that made it to Gangnam's Tehran
Boulevard.

"What has to happen will happen," Jae said, and raced to the front again.

Mokran and I hesitated before following him. The rest of the group whooped as they trailed after Jae. The police had set up a barricade of triangular cones across the Hannam Bridge's entry point, but Jae swerved onto the sidewalk to avoid it.

He had no idea that there was a reward on his head. Some police tried to stop him, then retreated. When the car-*pok* saw the barricade, they halted, but over a thousand bikes continued to race after Jae and head for Hannam Bridge. Jae didn't know this, but Seoul's entire traffic police force was gathering around that bridge.

To Jae, the cones that the police often used for barricades were symbolic obstacles. If they were truly annoying, you could just get off the bike and move them. The waiting police headed straight for Jae. He eluded them in any way he could, followed by hundreds of bikes that had also detoured around the barricade of cones. In the ensuing chaos, the conscripted police fell into total panic. The rally's front guard, driving cars, had gotten out to clear the barricade for the others. Then they began fighting with the police.

When the barricade was finally cleared, around a thousand bikers honked their horns and charged across the bridge. Confronted by the tsunami of motorcycles, the young policemen — simply fulfilling military duty — became terrified and retreated to their checkpoint. The car-*pok* waiting at the shoulder of the road started moving again. The rally triumphantly passed Hannam Bridge and sped toward the Yanjae main road. There was nothing blocking the way to Tehran Boulevard.

37

PYO WATCHED THE SCENE UNFOLD. HE SAID LIST-
lessly to Seungtae, "They got through."

"The next meeting point must be Tehran Boulevard. The kids that crossed Dongho Bridge and the ones that crossed Hannam will merge and turn the area inside out," Seungtae said while checking a text message. "Now they're saying, 'Bitches, stop them at all costs!'"

Outbursts of anger had started up again in the control room. Seungtae turned down the walkie-talkie's volume.

Pyo asked, "What do we do?"

"They'll return north across the river for sure," said Seungtae. "They'll end where they began. Maybe Jongno or Jongmyo or Gwanghwamun. Those are good places for them to break up later because of all the possible escape routes and alleys. Even if we can't get many of the kids tonight, at the very least we've got to get that guy Jae. If we don't manage to get him this time, he'll grow even stronger and by the next Independence Movement Day, we'll have an even more uncontrollable number of bikes creating havoc."

A new order came through on Seungtae's walkie-talkie. He made his disapproval clear, saying, "That's too dangerous. I can't be responsible for that."

So many orders were coming from different places — the chain of command itself needed traffic control. If problems surfaced, whoever had been at the scene could end up taking the blame. Soon the final order came in. Seungtae conveyed it to his subordinates, who asked the same question he had. Who would be held responsible if something went wrong?

A report came in that the rally was now heading north. Seungtae already knew which bridge they would cross. Seongsu. They could be taking Yangjae Highway north, but at a certain juncture they would have to shift and cross Seongsu Bridge. Once again the police set up a barricade.

38

AS BEFORE, JAE DIDN'T TAKE THE POLICE BARRI-
cade seriously, but as he approached Seongsu Bridge from the
south, he saw that this one was different. It was the first time the
police were using the steel-spiked barricade on the motorcycle
gangs. Jae had never seen or heard of it — one of the limitations
of being an eighteen-year-old leader.

I tried to stop Jae. "I don't think it's a good idea to cross."

"Why?"

"I have a bad feeling about this."

"I can hear it," Jae said, as if he had spoken to an oracle.

"What?"

"What the bridge is thinking. And what the river's saying to
me."

"What's it saying?"

"They're calling me," Jae said. "They're telling me it's where
I have to go."

He suddenly frowned and clutched his chest.

Mokran asked, "What's wrong?"

He took deep breaths and leaned against the handlebars until his forehead nearly rested against the dashboard. The pain
seemed to be worsening.

"Are you hurt?" Mokran asked. She began approaching him,
but Jae raised his hand and stopped her. He straightened up.

"I'm better. It happens now and then."

Jae glanced back at the motorcycle rally he was leading. He frowned as if he was still feeling pain, but he grabbed the handlebars, his mind made up. Jae rode up the bridge with the front guard. Mokran followed. The patrol car's high beams were aimed at Jae and bathed him in light so strong, it was difficult to open your eyes, but Jae didn't retreat. Police holding megaphones shouted warnings that if he didn't stop, he would be arrested. The conscripted police came in one line at Jae, their batons raised.

Nearly halfway across Seongsu Bridge, a spike punctured his motorcycle tire. The bike wobbled and skidded to the road like a rolling coin that had lost momentum, then teetered. Jae's Honda hit the concrete median strip, flew into the bridge railing, and then his body soared over the water like a balloon a child had let go.

Jae spun in the air. The mouth of the wide, black river, the brightly lit bridges, the police car lights, and the red brake lights all entered his eyes. His spirit was escaping his body, and it felt different from anything he had ever known. He sensed that he could be gone for a very long time, wandering restlessly without settling, and be transformed into a completely new being.

He no longer felt the force of gravity. There was no velocity to the fall, no cold water, no fear of suffocation. He was slowly rising. Looking down, he saw the bridge below. The dozens of motorcycles that had followed him charged the police barriers and skidded with flat tires to the ground. Mokran, Gas Tank, and Seesaw Eyes fell too. Mokran's face was soaked in blood and she writhed in pain on the asphalt. She tried reaching out, but her body wasn't listening. It was as if her physical self no longer existed. The motorcycle rally, with its advance blocked, turned southward. It resembled a twitching worm covered in salt. Now greedy for victory, the police forced their way across the bridge. When I turned, in the distance I saw the Express Bus Terminal where Jae had been born. The buses ready to leave at daybreak sounded so close by, it was as if their engines were idling next to me. I thought then that maybe Jae's soul would lie down and finally find peace at the terminal.

39

A WITNESS SAID, "AT FIRST I DIDN'T EVEN KNOW IT

was Jae. Someone just rose up into the air. I mean it, shit, maybe I'm losing my mind."

Hundreds of motorcycle gangs on the Seongsu Bridge over-pass that day claimed they saw Jae ascend to the heavens. They said that rays beamed down from the sky and carried him up. Their testimonies lined up. Around three in the morning they saw a vague shape rising in a sudden path of light; they were sure that this was Jae. Some of the drafted police officers also posted online about seeing the same thing, with comments like "He spread his white wings and rose into the sky. It was definitely Jae. He had longish hair, and he was tall and thin."

The only pictures were cell-phone shots of a dark, blurry sky. Some photographed an indistinct light in the pictures, but that was all. Many on the Olympic Highway also saw the phenom-enon from their cars. Some Catholics asserted that it was the Virgin Mother appearing on August 15, the feast day of the As-sumption.

Seungtae had also been on Seongsu Bridge. He saw Jae's miserable expression when his long hair had parted, fluttering in the wind. When the boy and his motorcycle had gone over the bridge handrail toward the water, Seungtae closed his eyes.

"Ascension?" said Seungtae the next day to the chief of security. "Do you believe everything you read on the Internet? I'm telling you, it didn't happen."

He added, "Wasn't I there? It's impossible for it to happen right in front of my eyes and for me not to see it."

The chief of security picked at his ear. "You think an ascension happens in front of your eyes? It probably happened over your head."

A diving team found the submerged motorcycle but never discovered the body. The next day the police briefed the press on the Liberation Day motorcycle rally. One missing, 6 bikers injured, 15 police injured, 127 arrested. The gist was that swift, thorough police action at the rally had subdued a potentially large-scale public disturbance in its early stages. Still, alongside news articles titled THE MADNESS OF MOTORCYCLE RALLIES: HOW LONG WILL THEY TEST US? were critical articles with titles like EXTREME POLICE ACTION LEADS TO HUMAN RIGHTS VIOLATIONS CONTROVERSY. Related articles exploded all over the Internet and hundreds of commenters offered their opinions. Hatred ran like a river. But within a few days the articles were crowded out by other news as people lost interest in the motorcycle rally. Summer was coming to an end, and tourists returning from their travels waited for taxis at Incheon International Airport, holding duty-free shopping bags.

PART
FIVE

FOUR YEARS AGO, I FIRST HEARD ABOUT THE BOY

named Jae from a girl I'd dated for a year during college. Let's call her Y. She was a freshman in my school literature club who, in contrast to her quick-witted, energetic appearance, was sensitive and kindhearted. I was more interested in novels, but she liked poetry. We didn't keep in touch after graduating, then years later, she e-mailed me after reading an article about a novel I'd written.

When I called the phone number she'd sent me, she was pleased to hear from me and said she hadn't been sure she'd had the right e-mail address. She had been passionate about politics as a student, and after graduating had worked for an NGO. Then she got a job making Korean-language teaching manuals for an educational publisher. After working there for some time, she left and was now at an organization that helped at-risk youth. She said she had read my novel.

"So I saw I was in your novel." She was sure that one of the characters in the book was based on her.

"I don't think so," I disagreed, laughing.

"I'm sure it's me."

"You keep insisting, though the writer says you're wrong."

"Do writers always know everything about their own books? You might have written about me without knowing it."

Okay, let's leave it at that, I thought, and backed off. And she was right about one thing: a writer doesn't have complete control over his own novel. I was curious, so I asked, "So which one are you?"

"I don't think that's for me to say."

Which character in my book resembled her? She refused to tell me, so I resorted to guessing. I could find her if I looked, but it seemed a waste of energy, considering that sometimes even readers who've never met the writer will assert that a character was based on them. Someone once said that a person remembers his life, at most, only a little more vividly than the memory of a novel he has read. I was actually more interested in my fading memories of the year we had dated than the character she resembled.

I asked, "Are you married?"

She hesitated, then said that she and her husband had separated. They didn't have children. It turned out that I knew her husband; we had briefly been members of the same university club. He had seemed rather cynical and cold, and looked like a model student, but lewd rumors about his relationships with women never ceased throughout college. Y didn't seem to want to talk about him and started talking about her job instead. She said she visited the biker kids that gathered under the Wonhyo Bridge weekly to counsel them. Her organization had done this work for years, and also ran a shelter where runaway teenagers could stay for a short time.

"If you're ever curious about what we do, come on over. Our volunteers are really lovely people."

I didn't know then that this was a half-open door.

I asked, "Is there anything you need for the shelter?"

"Well, our fax machine broke a while ago. If you've got one

idling at home, could you donate it to us? I know no one uses them anymore, but we do."

There was an old flea market near my neighborhood, so I bought a used fax machine at a stall between Sindang Market and Seongdong Technical High School, and paid her a visit. The second floor of the Western-style house had been remodeled into a shelter where runaway teenagers could sleep, and the first floor was used as an office for the volunteers.

The volunteers, all in their early twenties, were openly curious about their boss's ex-boyfriend dropping by at the office. They seemed to like me even more once I offered up the fax machine and tangerines. We peeled the tangerines and chatted, but the cheerful atmosphere soon turned. Y's organization was having financial problems. I could have guessed — they couldn't even afford a used fax machine. Municipal funding had dwindled, and there were few companies that donated to causes for runaways and abused teenagers since it didn't help their image.

I took a look at their newsletter. "I was always interested in this area of work."

Y said, "Really?"

"I once wrote a short story called 'Emergency Exit.' Have you read it? A story about teenage burglars."

"Oh, that one. It was kind of shocking. What kind of fiction starts like that?"

She shuddered in mock horror. She was still the Y I remembered, but her appearance had changed. Back then she had been a chubby-faced student in her early twenties. But the Y in front of me was an emaciated middle-aged lady with sunken cheeks. It was strange, unfamiliar. It felt like I was meeting an actress playing the role of Y.

"Well, you probably see a lot worse here," I said.

"Yeah, but reading it in a novel's more shocking. Literature somehow seems like it should be about something more refined . . . You know what I mean."

"I wrote that story then actually shoved it in a drawer for six months," I said. "I never thought I'd be able to publish it. There were days when I couldn't write a single sentence. Then, when it looked like I'd miss my deadline altogether, I showed the story to a friend. My friend read it and told me to try to publish it right away, so I drummed up the courage and sent it to the magazine. Back then no one was writing stories about these kinds of kids."

"What inspired you to write it?" she asked.

"You remember the War on Crime, or whatever it was called during Roh Tae-woo's regime when they suddenly banned alcohol after midnight?"

"Yes," she said. "The Prohibition period. Remember how once it hit midnight, the touts owned the world? They lured you in, saying, *Older Sister, Older Brother, have another drink.* Then they brought you to a secret basement bar three floors down, where you couldn't leave till four in the morning, and in that smoked-filled space you had to hand over a chunk of money to drink."

"There was that famous tout called Green Pillow, a girl who went around with a green pillow tucked under her arm. People were mesmerized by that pillow and followed it everywhere, into beer halls and *soju* bars, but when you got there, she disappeared to go out and bait other customers. I started writing 'Emergency Exit' one night after I saw that green pillow."

Y said cautiously, "You'll probably find good material if you write a book about our kids. Why don't you try it? We'll help you."

People often say that a single novel can't do justice to one's own life story, but writers are more interested in a life they feel able to write about than in representing the sheer variety of lives. But I enthusiastically agreed, if only to be polite. "Really? If there's an interesting kid, why don't you put us in touch?"

The volunteers around us spoke up at the same time: "You should meet Donggyu."

"Is he also a biker kid?"

Y said, "He was . . . He doesn't ride anymore."

I knew that traitors and defectors often had interesting stories, so I was suddenly intrigued, and asked them to pick a date for us to meet.

Donggyu worked part-time at a gas station, and gave me the impression of being dark and unsociable. He seemed like a kid who lived with his heart locked up. If Y hadn't accompanied us the first time, it's likely that Donggyu would have refused to meet me. As soon as Y saw Donggyu she gave him a hug. He wasn't startled and instead threw open his arms and hugged her back. It reminded me of a long-ago memory of Y and myself. We used to call the hill near our university's east gate Turgenev Hill. Word was that the poet Yun Dong-ju used to like that hill, but that's never been confirmed. From the hill sparsely dotted with pine trees you saw cars passing on the road in front of the women's university, and in spring, azaleas would bloom, then lilacs. We would climb the rarely visited hill, holding each other and sometimes kissing.

She had no idea what I was thinking as she introduced me to Donggyu. He merely nodded casually at me. Y left quickly as she had things to take care of, and Donggyu and I went to get pizza. At first it was awkward, but I waited. I've learned that introverts speak in more depth and more frankly once they get going.

He asked me, "What would you like to talk about?"

"Well . . . anything you want, really."

He looked suspiciously my way, but the look quickly faded. We chatted, though our conversation didn't progress very far. Still, I left sensing that he had something to say, and that he was determined to keep our dialogue going. When I suggested meeting again, Donggyu agreed. A week later, I returned to the gas station and we continued our interview at the pizza parlor. I asked him about his childhood, and listened to him talk about his aphonia, his mother's infidelity, his father's second marriage, and the conflicts that had continued to follow him. But gradually he began talking less about himself and kept returning to his friend Jae's story.

"Why do you keep talking about Jae?" I asked. "I want to hear your story . . ."

"Jae is me," he said.

"What do you mean?"

"I don't know. It's hard to explain, but I need to talk about Jae."

Donggyu kept a diary, which is rare for a teenage boy. And it wasn't just the diary — he had a habit of keeping a record of everything, so he was able to faithfully recount his childhood as if he were reciting from a book. Sometimes he riffled through his notebook when he wasn't sure of a year or day, but otherwise he never corrected himself. Basically, he had a trustworthy memory.

I met him two more times after that. The last time we met, I checked in with him again. "So everything I've heard so far, I can use in a novel?"

"Yes, someone has to write Jae's story."

"Why?"

"Jae once said that someone would write his story someday."

"Don't you think that person was supposed to be you?"

"Maybe. But Jae being who he was, he wouldn't have wanted it to be someone like me just jotting his life into a diary. Jae really believed he was doing great things. He believed he was painting on a canvas of the universe with thousands of motorcycles. He thought it was a real art form. I mean, even the solar eclipse is a kind of art. Even though the moon only blocks the sun for a little while, people come from all over the world to see it."

"A form of performance art or environmental art," I said. "I think that's what you're talking about. Do you really think Jae knew about these kinds of things?"

"He read a lot of books. You know how people throw away all kinds of books these days. He probably knew about performance art — he was really sharp. And he wasn't a con man."

Donggyu gasped like a kid with a heart problem, but struggled to keep speaking. "I . . . I never talk about this since people will think I'm crazy."

"What is it?"

"I keep hearing Jae's voice."

"What does he say?"

"Nothing new. I hear him saying things he used to say, like a tape recorder."

"I sometimes hear characters from my novels talking. I'll sit and be staring at nothing when I think I hear someone talking to me. I'll turn around, but no one'll be there. Now that I think about it, I wrote this very dialogue down a few days ago."

Donggyu looked upset and hurt because he hadn't been understood.

"His voice is vivid to me, vivid enough to wake me up when I'm sleeping. Sometimes I'll walk down the street and hear him."

"What do you hear most often?"

"I hear, 'What has to happen will happen.'"

"Jae once said that, didn't he? What do you think it means?"

"I'm not sure. But each time I hear him say that, for some reason I feel as if he's forgiving me."

I met Mokran next, at a hospital. She had been with Jae up to his last moment, until her optic nerve was pierced by the sharp steel barricade. It had left her blind in her right eye. The doctor had told her it was a miracle that her left eye was still intact. She was visiting the hospital regularly for checkups and rehab. After producing repeated box-office flops, her father had stopped making movies and was now in the middle of suing the government and the police department for use of excessive force. I wanted to meet him but he never responded to me.

Mokran wasn't too different from the way that Donggyu had

described her. It was hard to see her as a perfect beauty, but she had a unique, asymmetrical look about her that got your attention. She was somehow different from other girls, who were all starting to look alike.

Mokran asked me, "What are you looking for?"

"Nothing special, nothing in particular."

"That's a load of shit."

She rejected all attempts at serious conversation. She had heard a lot about people who "hunted" for stories from her father. People who dug for every single word of your story, but, after they manipulated it as they pleased and turned it into a movie, they turned their back on you. So how could she know I wasn't that kind of person? Especially when I didn't even know myself very well.

I said, "Donggyu already told me everything there is to know."

"So why did you come meet me?"

"Well, there were some things I didn't feel comfortable asking him."

Only then did she look interested.

I asked, "Where was Donggyu at the very end?"

We went to the wide patio on the third floor.

She said, "You don't have any cigarettes on you, do you?"

"No, I quit smoking."

"What kind of writer doesn't smoke?"

"Should I get you some?"

"Yes."

"What kind?"

"Marlboro."

When I returned with the cigarettes, Mokran had disappeared. I repeatedly tried the phone number for her that Dong-gyu had given me, but she didn't pick up. I decided not to bother Mokran anymore. The pack of Marlboros is still on my desk.

I began writing the first part of my novel based on what Donggyu had told me and had written down himself. Jae's appearance and Donggyu's aphonia belonged to another part of the book. Up to that point the writing was easy, but after that I got stuck. I ended up putting it aside and focusing on another book. About a year later, I decided that this novel was also going nowhere so I filed it away in a drawer.

I started wondering if I should seek out Lieutenant Pak Seungtae. From a bulletin board at Y's organization, I learned that he would be participating in a symposium about teenage motorcycle gangs, where professors of education and NGO workers, former bikers turned university students, and police would discuss potential countermeasures.

Lieutenant Pak was a stocky man in his mid-thirties. His face was angular and his leather biking jacket resembled a suit of armor. His official duties concerned foreign affairs, but he often assisted with work related to teen motorcycle gangs because he cared deeply about them. Capable police officers talented in foreign languages are often posted in the Foreign Affairs Division, and people in those positions often glowed with pride. I'd seen on the Internet that the media had often interviewed Lieutenant Pak about motorcycle gangs. So he didn't seem guarded, though I'd introduced myself as a writer who wanted to interview him.

He handed me his business card. "Which part are you most interested in?"

He looked friendly but his eyes were sharp. A byproduct of his job.

"I'd like to hear about Jae."

"Who?" His expression changed into a complex mix of suspicion, alarm, and a little disappointment.

"You didn't know anyone named Jae?"

He frowned. "I don't know what kind of rumors you've heard, but I don't know a Jae."

"Do you mean you didn't know him personally, or that you don't know anyone by that name at all?"

He looked at me for a long time, as if trying to read my mind, then gave a short sigh. "Are you really a fiction writer?"

"Yes, would you like me to send you a few copies of my books?"

"Are you thinking of writing a novel about this?"

"I'll be fictionalizing it," I said. "People accept what fiction writers write as fiction."

"Well, if you're interested in the rumors floating around, I have a thing or two I can tell you . . ."

"I'd also appreciate your help in understanding the teen motorcycle gang culture."

When I called him the next day, his attitude had changed. After he had looked me up on the Internet and done a bit of research, he became a little nicer. He had learned that I wasn't a nonfiction writer planning an exposé. We met at a bar that sold fishcakes and got to talking. When I gave him a few of my novels as gifts, he put them casually into his bag without asking me to sign them, saying, "I'll read them. Thanks."

Our conversation naturally focused on Jae. Pak gave me a detailed summary of what he knew about him.

"Have you met Donggyu? His father is a cop, part of our family. When I put out a call for information on our intranet server, he responded. When we met he told me that Jae's family had once rented from them, and that his son and Jae were friends. From there it was easy to pin down Jae's identity. There's a rumor that Jae's not even real, but that's not true. He definitely existed. Anyway, before Liberation Day we dug around everywhere, trying to arrest him. Of course, we first hauled in Donggyu. He was very cooperative."

"Why did he cooperate with the police, when Jae was his friend?"

"He thought it was the only way to help Jae. He said that Jae was starting to lose his grip on reality. You must've heard that he even attacked a police station. He didn't tolerate upstarts and was merciless with them. Donggyu seemed to believe that Jae was lost in delusions of grandeur, and he had to be put back in his place. In his own way, Donggyu was trying to help him. But this is where it stops."

"Where what stops?"

"I mean everything up to this point is true. The stuff after — from breaching police lines and falling into the Han River and rising up to heaven — that's all nonsense. You're not going to put that in the novel, are you? But since it's a novel, I guess you could. Yes, put it in. It doesn't matter."

I said, "Jae definitely reached Seongsu Bridge, correct? And you're saying that you don't believe what happened afterward."

"That's right."

"So where has Jae gone, then?"

"He's probably hidden himself somewhere. He's perfectly capable of that. You know he's a wanted man. The way he was born is strange. There's even something odd about the fire that broke out while he was at the orphanage. Then when he moved up to Seoul he became a loner, roamed around homeless, and later, ate raw rice. He could be disguised as a homeless person right now. And at first glance, he does pass for a grown man."

"To what extent did Donggyu cooperate?"

"Since all the groups got mixed up during the rally, it was important for us to know where Jae's group was moving. So Donggyu stuck close to Jae and kept us updated with his movements."

"So you really didn't see anything at the bridge? Hundreds of patrol officers said they did, and weren't you in the very front?"

Lieutenant Pak snorted. "You have quite an imagination."

He downed a shot of *soju*. "Let me ask you one favor. What you write is up to you, but I'm asking you, please, don't glorify the biker gangs. They're really pitiful kids. Don't you think I know how they feel? There isn't a soul in the country who understands them the way I do. But it's dangerous. Kids paralyzed head to toe, you think I haven't seen it more than a few times? It's all temporary insanity."

We continued meeting up for drinks. Despite his initial prickliness, he had a gentle side to him. On days he had too much, he told me his deepest thoughts, which I hadn't expected.

"There's going to be a character based on you in my novel. Is that okay?" I finally asked.

"As long as people can't immediately tell it's me, I guess it's fine."

Of course, even without his permission, I would have inserted him into the novel in some way. Before we parted, I asked him something I'd been wanting to ask for some time. "Do you feel guilty about what happened to Jae? I mean, there's a strong chance he's dead. And that police barricade caused real damage. One kid lost her vision and many others were injured."

He stared at me. "First, it wasn't my decision alone. Our policy is to be firm in the face of collective action that disturbs the peace or harms the public. The kids knew what to expect. The second they go without a helmet, they're inviting death. It probably appeals to the cocky young ones, anyway. Do you remember that educational program about trying to get helmets on them? Ridiculous, isn't it? But there's one more thing I want to say to you, Mr. Fiction Writer."

"What is it?"

"I — no, the entire police force — was an absolutely essential presence."

"For what? Do you mean to keep the public order?"

"No, not that. I thought you'd know, since you're a writer. It wasn't a case of being at the wrong place at the wrong time, but we were where we needed to be at the right time. We were able to carry out our duties."

"So you feel absolutely no guilt?"

"That's right."

He got up first. We shook hands, then parted. He was walking away with clipped steps when he suddenly turned back.

"Oh, there's one more thing I want to say." He ran his hand across his cropped hair. "I did see it."

"What?"

"Jae rising. To heaven, I mean." He pointed up at the sky.

"What do you think that's about?"

"It's always a crowd of people who see UFOs, right? I think it's something like that."

A group of noisy teenagers flooded us like an ocean wave. We shook hands in the middle of the chaos and parted again.

After that I met several members of motorcycle gangs, but I

only managed to collect more vague rumors about Jae. In contrast to the pile of research growing on my desk, my novel was going nowhere. I didn't know how to continue. The beginning alone I rewrote ten times, then quit. But I continued jotting down notes whenever something came to me. A year passed, but even when I ended up leaving to live abroad for a bit, my story about Jae went nowhere.

Then one day I received a short e-mail message from Y in Seoul. It said that Donggyu, whose father had persuaded him to return home, had been studying for the civil service exam. He had stayed up late one night on the phone talking to Mokran, then mixed pills into a bottle of *soju* and killed himself.

I took my unfinished novel out of its drawer and placed it on the desk. The manuscript sat there like an unwanted guest. It felt wrong to continue after what had happened to Donggyu. I flipped through, intending to reread the novel, but I couldn't bring myself to read the scenes related to him, so I put it down. I felt ashamed that after all our conversations together, I hadn't been able to stop his death. Was fiction — and, by extension, the writer — capable of doing anything?

A few idle months passed. The American sculptor Steven De Staebler once said, "Artists don't get down to work until the pain of working is exceeded by the pain of not working." I opened that drawer again only when I got to the point where I couldn't bear not writing anymore. I reread the notes I'd taken, and I began writing to a word count every day. I gained momentum. Flowers bloomed in the spring, disappeared, and summer began. When summer began to fade, I took a look at the novel and saw I had nearly enough material for two books. I felt disturbed, but I couldn't pinpoint why. I just needed to keep writing and fill a set quota of pages per day. I rubbed out the uneasy embers deep inside me and silently wrote toward my quota.

"Is it going well?" Y asked on our first phone call in ages. After listening quietly to my situation for a bit, she said, "Just listen."

"To what?"

"They'll talk, won't they? Your characters, I mean. You need to be quiet and just listen to them."

It was as if a heavy weight had been lifted, and outside of the main characters' story lines, I decided to throw away the rest. It was like starting all over again. I restructured the novel without veering away too much from what Donggyu had written. As soon as I got rid of the narrative strands I'd added to the novel, I was able to breathe again. My manuscript nearly shrank in half. I saw gaps in the story, but I decided to leave it as it was. Making a perfect narrative didn't seem to suit the story. As soon as I had a draft, I sent it to Y.

"Can you read through it once for me? If you tell me not to send it in, I won't. You can be more objective than me. If it's going to be a problem for the kids, I'll give up on it for good."

A few days later Y responded. She said she had read the manuscript and didn't think it would cause them problems. The interesting thing was her postscript: "By the way, one of our volunteers knows that you're writing a novel about Jae's life. She asked for your e-mail address, so I passed it on. Is that okay? You'll probably receive an e-mail soon."

A few days later a woman who called herself Jean contacted me. She said that she wanted to tell me a story about Jae; I opened the file she had attached to the e-mail and read to the end. Jae was vivid in a way that I hadn't seen in any other interviews or documents about him. At first I thought I would insert it into the novel somewhere, but it was hard to find a natural place for it, and I didn't think it was necessary to the novel's arc, so I am adding it here:

In April, on a day that felt more like winter, a woman went to throw out the trash and discovered a young man crouched by the wall surrounding her house. She thought he might have frozen to death so she stood at his feet for some time, when his shoes began to wiggle. The boy sensed her there, but barely managed to open his eyes. He looked up with the gaze of a stray cat hoping for something to eat. The exact angle of his gaze was a coincidence; the teenage boy and the woman met just after her cat had died of an inflamed intestine.

The woman said, "Let's go in. After you warm up, we'll get you some food."

She led him indoors and gave him a meal with some soup. He ate a total of five eggs that she fried up for him. After he thawed out, he took a shower and then fell asleep on the sofa. He spent several days at her house until he recovered his energy. A glow returned to his cheeks and he steadily gained weight. Then one night, he stole her wallet and valuables, and fled. She called to cancel her credit card, but in that short time he had already used it to purchase some clothes in the Myeongdong shopping district.

"Where did you lose your card?" the operator asked the woman.

She lied and said she had lost her wallet while out. She was baffled by how the teenager, whom she had treated kindly, had suddenly reverted to burglary. She disliked easy answers such as "Human beings are fundamentally dishonest." But in avoiding the obvious conclusions, other perplexing questions weighed down on her like heavy moving boxes. She was frustrated and felt wronged but she suppressed her feelings. She didn't want to be like her mother, who always blamed others. There were solutions available for an educated girl. No matter how difficult, she couldn't give up. If she gave up, she would become the kind of woman her mother was, so she went to the hospital instead. The psychiatrist prescribed antidepressants to the woman, who had developed insomnia. She decided to trust the medication approved by the American FDA.

A year passed and then it was spring again. She was returning home after an evening appointment when she stopped in front of her house. A teenager was crouched asleep against her brick wall. What was this? Was life mocking her? At first she thought the young thief from the year before had returned. The way this boy slept, with his face buried in his knees, and his posture and his shoulders, reminded her of him. She stared at the boy, then rushed into the house. He didn't wake up; he could even be dead. She glanced out occasionally while working but from where she was, she couldn't see over the wall. The temperature difference was extreme during the changing seasons, and as it got dark, the temperature dropped.

Near midnight she called her mother. "Mom, it's me."

"What time is it?"

"Were you asleep?"

Her mother said, "I was just lying down after doing some grading."

"How are the students this year?"

"At this time of night? What's wrong?"

"It's nothing."

Her mother said, "Some experiences are better left alone."

"Why're you saying that all of a sudden?"

"I don't know what the problem is, but it's best not to do anything you're unsure about."

"You're worrying over nothing. Please don't act like you've got some sixth sense. Mom, you just don't."

"But I do have it."

"I just called because I suddenly thought of you. That's all, so go to sleep."

"Forgive your husband. That's the humane thing to do."

The woman hurled her cell phone at the sofa and screamed and screamed.

She switched off the TV and lay down. Her heart was drumming so fast, she was unable to sleep. She popped a tranquilizer and returned to bed, but instead of calming down she just became dizzier. The sound of wind rattling the windowpanes grew louder. She thought about the kid huddled up against the wall, and wondered if she should just call the cops.

To someone racked with insomnia, morning seems an eternity away. It feels as if you're a defendant summoned to court every day. On good days a trial doesn't take place, but you still have to appear in court. The prosecutor of this lawyer-free cross-examination is the self. And the relentless interrogation that always seems at the cusp of ending doesn't actually end until dawn. The process repeats itself night after night. No matter how often you experience insomnia, you never get used to it. Each time the woman lay sleepless, she wondered if she was actually living in what Christians called purgatory.

She sprang up and went outside. The boy hadn't budged and was still huddled against the wall. She poked his shoulder with her finger.

"Hey, kid!" she said.

He shuddered and looked up.

She saw that the face lit up by the street lamp wasn't the same kid. Instead of relief, she felt vaguely disappointed.

"Who are you?" she asked. "What are you doing here like this? Are you going to stay here all night?"

He said nothing.

"You keep this up and you'll freeze to death. It doesn't just happen in winter."

"I'm sorry," he said. "I'll go elsewhere."

"Let's go in," she said, just as she had a year ago. "Let's get you warmed up and get you something to eat."

"That's all right, *ajumma*. I'm fine."

"I'm not all right with it. Don't protest. Come in. Quick!"

He stood up. He straightened his joints, stiff from being crouched so long, like an old umbrella being opened. She almost heard them creaking.

"I said it's fine," he said. "I've got places to go."

He stubbornly shook his head and walked around, as if trying to regain his sense of direction.

"Why sleep here if you have somewhere to go?" she persisted. "Have you been drinking?"

"No."

She shivered as the wind cut through the stitching of her knit cardigan.

"I'm too cold for this. Come inside, quick."

She took his arm and tugged him toward the house. Only then, still hesitating, he limped in. She hadn't been aware of it, but once inside she smelled the violent stench coming from him. It was as if the sewer system itself had entered the house. She heated up some frozen dumplings and served them to him with hot citron tea. He finished off the dumplings in one swallow and then emptied the wicker basket of tangerines set on the coffee table in no time. She furtively studied him while preparing more food. It felt good to watch him eat until his cheeks were stuffed, but the kid she met a year ago had been the same. This one could steal her wallet at any time and run off to wherever he had come from.

She said, "What's your name?"

"Why do you want to know?"

"You don't have a name?"

"Doesn't everyone have a name?"

"So I'm asking you your name. Why, is there a reason you can't tell me your name?"

Was he mixed up in some crime? She gently picked up the knife set on the counter and put it back in a drawer.

"I'm Jae."

"It's a nice name." It could be a fake name.

"Have you warmed up?" She approached the sofa where he was sitting and examined him. He had a face that was hard to judge.

"Yes, but *ajumma* . . ."

"What is it? Do you want more tea?"

"I don't want to be rude, but can I watch TV for a second?"

"There's something on you want to watch at this time?" she said. "It's dawn."

"The Premier League from England. There's going to be a match on."

"What's that?"

"Soccer. You don't watch?"

"Not really. I'm hopeless at sports."

"It's Manchester against Arsenal. It's a big game."

"That's fine, but take a shower first. Then you can watch TV."

Jae stared into the face of the woman telling him to shower. She understood immediately what his look meant: he was looking for any hidden motives on her part. She avoided his eyes and said, "You smell terrible."

"I don't have anything to change into."

"I've got clothes. I don't know if they'll fit you, but I'll leave them beside the bathroom."

She felt a compelling, almost instinctive desire to put Jae's dirty clothes in the washing machine. It was as if her heart would become lighter once she saw the dirty water gurgle down the drain. But that meant the kid couldn't leave right away. She briefly regretted telling him to shower, then shook her head and tossed Jae's discarded clothes into the machine, took what the other kid had left a year ago from the closet, and set them by the bathroom.

Afterward Jae said, "They're a little big for me."

He stopped drying his hair and looked around as if he expected to see another man present. The woman pointed at the television. The sportscasters had started discussing the imminent match. Jae, whose entire body had turned pink from the hot shower, sat on the sofa. The shower had relaxed him and he smiled, ate the strawberries that she brought over, and became absorbed in the match. She suddenly felt like she was floating as she watched him — similar but different from when she overdosed on anti-depressants. It felt as if someone were injecting her with a chemical happiness through the gap at the tip of her big toe. She wasn't sure why she felt such star-tling happiness watching a stranger — a teenage boy — eat her food and watch a match taking place far away. These intense feelings also made her anxious. If a balloon lost all its air, gravity was sure to pull her down and hurl her back to the harsh world. Just like it had a year ago.

"Hey, kid," she said.

Jae, who'd been lost in the match, turned when she called. "Yes?"

"You should leave now. I want you to leave."

"What? Right now?" He looked confused. "What about my clothes?"

"What do you mean, your clothes?"

"You took them a little while ago, saying you're go-ing to wash them."

She slapped her forehead. "Oh, those. I'm wash-ing them right now."

"Then what should I do?"

"You're right. Stay put for now. But you'll have to go as soon as your clothes are dry. Understand? I'm sorry, I'm really sorry."

"It's all right. I was thinking of doing that anyway." His tone was polite but cold. "I would've left right away if you hadn't taken my clothes."

"Right," she said. "I'm sorry, I forgot. But it's nice to have clean clothes, isn't it?"

"That's true."

"Keep watching the soccer match. I'll let you know when your clothes are dry. It'll be quick, with the dryer."

"Okay. It's fine if they're not totally dry." Jae turned back to the TV, where the players were moving behind the ball as if they were dancing.

She smoked in the backyard and strengthened her resolve to send him away as soon as his clothes dried. She wouldn't be forced back to a life of taking antidepressants.

When she returned to the living room, the first half of the match had ended.

He asked, "*Ajumma*, do you live alone?"

She lied. "No."

"Then with who?"

"Well, he just stepped out. He'll be back soon."

She tied back her disheveled, coarse hair with a rubber band.

"*Ajumma*, what do you do for a living?"

"Me? I work in publishing as a freelancer."

"What does 'freelancer' mean?"

"It means I work from home."

She pointed at the proofs on her desk, along with the highlighters and Post-its. Then she said, "You don't have a home?"

"No."

She didn't push further. She made fresh coffee and sliced some bread. She chopped up vegetables, drizzled them with olive oil, and placed a cherry tomato on top. As if he were her son, Jae calmly remained on the sofa and, without tearing his eyes away from the screen, accepted the salad. It felt good, seeing him like this. He concentrated on the match until the second half ended. Manchester won. As the match ended and commercials started up, Jae began falling asleep, his body tilting to the side until he was finally curled into a ball. She got a blanket and covered him.

She had assumed he was asleep when he whispered, "Thank you."

She went quietly to her room and read the manuscript she needed to send to the magazine by the end of the day. Normally she meticulously checked manuscripts two or three times, but not this time. She hastily tidied it up, and though there were several hours left until the deadline, she submitted it. Then she restlessly moved back and forth from her room to the living room, and stole glances at Jae. She lowered the curtains so the sunlight wouldn't disturb his sleep and she ignored the radio that she always kept on while she worked.

He didn't wake up until late afternoon. The house was blanketed with a heavy sleep. She had also returned to her room and lay down, immediately falling into her own deep, dream-filled nap. It was a dark dream. A girl approaches some cops that normally find her charming. When they see her white bloodstained clothes, they sense that something terrible has happened to her, but the girl is unable to speak. At the hospital they take her to, the doctor makes her open her mouth and examines her. It's probably to collect evidence. In the dream world, it seems like a perfectly natural act. Finally the cops receive word of the criminal's identity, so they don their heavy armor and go to find the suspect. The criminal turns out to be a fellow cop wearing the exact same armored outfit. They arrest him and drag him away like a dog. Mid-interrogation, the criminal suddenly rejects his fellow cops' questions, shoots upright, and fiercely erases the charge 'rape' written on the wall. He shouts, "I told you this isn't a rape case — it was assault!"

She opened her eyes. Jae was burrowing into her arms. Through the fog of sleepiness, she found herself pulling him up by his armpits. His body smelled of shampoo and soap. This calmed her a little, but when she felt his warm breath against her chin she realized that this scene wasn't a dream. Shocked, she shoved him away from her. It was too late. Jae skillfully fondled and caressed her. She kicked fiercely. As the alarm clock fell off the bedside table, the battery popped out.

Jae leaned into her ear and whispered, "*Ajumma*, I'm sorry. All you need to do is stay still. I'll do the rest."

I'll do the rest. Her body went limp at these words coming from a teenage boy young enough to still have his baby fat. Ethics are like an embankment. They protect you to a certain extent from an awakening, but when they collapse a flood follows. When she closed her eyes, she still faintly saw the teenage girl from her dream. The girl who desired revenge but couldn't speak. When she opened her eyes, she saw the boy flush with anticipation. It didn't immediately feel sinful, but she sensed that one corner of the life she had led was collapsing. She wasn't necessarily unhappy about it. She was about to let herself go when a critical voice exploded from inside her: "Some experiences are better left alone."

It wasn't a moral cry for an unconditional ban on sex with minors. This censor inside her resembled a judge at a religious trial more than a philosopher who had internalized a universal code of ethics. This judge was always taking issue with her pleasure-seeking. This judge was always the first to be critical of her when she started smoking, drinking, and realized that rubbing her crotch against the corner of her desk made her feel good. This judge also sounded like her mother. *Whatever happens is your fault*, the scolding voice said. *If you had behaved from the start, if you had controlled your filthy desires, nothing like this would have happened.* The stubborn detective who always had to find evidence from your past. The invisible torturer who exists without a physical presence and wouldn't let you sleep. The wily temptress who says that you could never escape this questioning until you die.

She grabbed her crotch, punched Jae in the chin, and screamed, "Stop! I told you stop! Stop, just stop!"

Jae halted. "I thought you'd like it."

"What kind of kid are you?"

He didn't respond. She pushed him off her. A hot stiffness passed across her thigh, but she pretended not to notice.

She adjusted her disheveled clothes. "It's all my fault."

"No, it's my fault."

"No, it's not that. I shouldn't have let you in from the start."

"I'm sorry."

"When a man and woman are in bed . . ." She stayed on the bed as she spoke. "They share this shameful moment. Do you hear what I'm saying?"

Her breath was still ragged.

"I think I get it."

"No, you don't. It didn't look like you did. You're supposed to do it with someone who's ready to share that shameful moment with you. It's no different from masturbation if you don't have that."

"I just wanted to stay here."

She said, "What are you talking about?"

He said, "I thought I had to do something for you if I stayed."

"That 'something' was this?"

"Yes."

"You, you've had experience."

Jae grinned in response.

The smile made her break out in goosebumps. She said coldly, "Go to the bathroom and take care of your business there. That'll clear your head."

"I'm fine now, really."

"Then straighten your clothes. Someone's coming."

"No one's going to come."

"How do you know?"

"I just know. It doesn't feel like you're really waiting for someone."

She wasn't lying when she said someone was coming, but she wasn't actually waiting for anyone either. Sometimes something else arrives instead of what we think we're waiting for, and is actually what we had truly wanted. Like this boy.

"You're an odd one. You don't feel like a kid, but you don't feel grown-up either."

"Really?"

They stayed quiet for a while. One of them sat at the head and the other at the foot of the bed. She said as casually as she could, "Actually, I'm sick."

"Where?"

"Here," she said as if she were talking about spraining her ankle, and pointed at her breast.

"What's wrong?"

"They say it's cancer."

"Cancer?"

When she used the word "cancer," it sounded as if she were handling a heavy bowling ball, but when Jae said it, it sounded like the name of a tropical fruit he had seen for the first time. She sensed a distinct difference in the weight of the words. It was probably an obscure, distant word to him, a planet in the galaxy. But it exists in my body, she thought. I can feel it, the lump of ominous cells settling in.

"Then what do you have to do?"

"They might have to remove it."

Jae moved forward on his knees toward her. She didn't stop him. He said, "This one?"

He pushed away her shirt collar with his long white fingers and held her breast in his hands. He looked as if he were mourning the imminent loss of a beloved object, and she felt comforted.

"Yes, that's the one."

"I see."

Jae gazed up at her, asking for permission. She nodded. He lowered his head and sucked at her nipple.

"Do as you please," she said. "It's not mine anymore."

"Then whose is it?"

"The hospital's. The minute they declared that there was a lump inside, it became theirs. My body's no longer mine."

"Then it's mine now."

"Fine, it's yours. Take it."

He took a deep breath as if he were a scuba diver entering the ocean, and sucked on her nipple again. It was quiet. It was as if the woman were soaking in a warm bath instead of becoming tight with sexual tension.

"When did you know," he said, "that it was cancer?"

"Two days ago."

"That's recent. You must have been shocked."

She thought about it. Had she been shocked? It was true that she hadn't thought of anything else all day long. "Yes, I was."

"But what exactly is cancer?"

"You don't know what cancer is?"

"Not exactly."

"Cancer's the uncontrollable growth of cells. Most cells know when it's their time to die, but not cancer cells. They just keep growing."

"It sounds like their energy — no, their will to live — is amazing. I make it sound like a computer game character."

"That's right. Cancer has a great will to live, but people die because of its terrifying will."

"Will you die too?"

"Everyone dies someday."

Jae shut his eyes tightly as if he were casting a spell on the disease, and began sucking on her nipple again. She looked down at the crown of his head where his hair bristled upward and cried a little. Were they tears of repentance, or of self-pity? As she was thinking about this, her nipple hardened. She pushed Jae off.

"You're pretty skilled. You have a girlfriend?"

He began telling her about everything that had happened to him on the streets. The teenagers who beat people up; the lawless, animalistic violence and sex; the abused girl and the kids who lived off her money. She stiffened with shock at the stories he recounted so calmly, and said, "I hadn't believed it when I saw things like that on the news."

Jae said sincerely, "Someone said that anything a human being can imagine eventually happens."

"Who said that?"

"A scientist on television."

"I assumed those kinds of things could happen," she said. "I just never imagined I would meet someone who'd been through it."

He said, "But you said you don't know even if it's growing inside you. Cancer, I mean. Kids like us, no one ever notices us either. We're invisible men — people just pass us by. It's probably because we make them feel disgusted and uncomfortable. If they can't take it, they just get rid of us."

Jae swept back his hair. She decided that she would take him to a hairdresser the next day.

"It's not good to belittle yourself," she said.

"What does 'belittle yourself' mean?"

"To put yourself down."

Jae smiled faintly. "I put it more mildly than what it's really like."

"You're a tough guy."

"I don't know about that, but I can't let myself be weak."

"My brother's stopping by soon," she said. "My younger brother."

"So someone is really coming over."

"We live together. He was out of town for a few days and is returning today."

She tucked her exposed breast back into her shirt. She felt irritable. It felt like a cold, alien object.

"Then, I'll leave now."

"Just stay."

"Really?"

"You guys might even get along. Or truly clash. You can say you've come to take art lessons from me. Oh, and also —"

"Yes?"

"Can you stop calling me *ajumma*?"

"What should I call you?"

"Everyone calls me Teacher Jean. My last name's Jean."

This is how her letter began. It kept going, with her brother coming home, Jae working part-time at her brother's store, and so on. I'm occasionally surprised at how people are so honest with fiction writers. What was it that made them feel as if they could trust me with their stories? Did they believe that once you crossed into the territory of fiction, their entire self became relative and newly defined? Or did they want to become a part of the cloud of myths surrounding Jae? The only certain thing was that she'd focused only on Jae in her writing — and for some reason she hadn't continued writing. Maybe her cancer spread, or maybe she'd come to think that what she knew of Jae wasn't enough.

Her Jae was slightly different from the one I'd imagined. The

Jae that she knew and the Jae that Donggyu had known could only be different. At the time she'd written about him, Jae had left Hanna's house and had essentially been homeless. And before Jae had shown up in front of Donggyu, chewing raw rice with the appearance of an ascetic, he had experienced a peaceful period at Teacher Jean's house.

I jotted down questions I wanted to ask her and e-mailed them off. Grouped together, they resembled a liturgical confession, especially the last question: "Do you believe that Jae is still alive and will return someday?"

She never replied.

Not long after, Mokran called me out of nowhere and told me she was soon leaving for Vancouver. I happened to be in Seoul for business. Her father wanted her to continue her studies before it was too late, and she had agreed. She asked me if I had time to briefly meet at the airport, and apologized for disappearing on me the last time without a word.

At Incheon Airport I saw that Mokran had put on some weight and her face had filled out. It suited her. She had on sunglasses to hide her glass eye. A large man, Mokran's father, appeared relieved that she was departing for Vancouver. In a low voice, he said, *Nothing good ever happened for her here.* He said he needed to exchange money and do some shopping, and then he left us alone.

Mokran said, "You asked me where Donggyu was last time we met."

The Mokran I'd written about in my novel was a teenager, but the Mokran in front of me had matured into a woman, so I responded using a polite, formal tone.

"Donggyu betrayed Jae," she said. "That's why he stayed behind, since he knew there was something waiting ahead."

"No, he wouldn't have known about that."

"How do you know?"

"I met the policeman that Donggyu was working with. Donggyu only texted him about where Jae was heading."

"Really? Then why did you want to meet me, when you already knew the story?"

"How did you know that Donggyu betrayed him?"

"Donggyu told me. After what happened to Jae, he showed up and whimpered to me every day at the hospital. There I was without an eye, and I was so angry seeing him whine like that. Once I even lost my temper. I wish I hadn't."

"Do you think Jae is still alive, somewhere?"

"Jae believed he could split his consciousness and enter someone else's — Donggyu thought that Jae was hiding somewhere inside a machine. He said Jae kept trying to speak to him. But I don't buy it. I think Jae killed himself. I think he knew that Donggyu turned him in."

Mokran's leg was shaking uncontrollably, and she kept crumpling up a napkin on the table.

"How do you feel when you look back on your motorcycle-riding days?"

"It was amazing, fucking amazing. But now, with only one eye, I've got no sense of spatial distance. When I think about how I'll never ride again, those times seem even more amazing. I still dream about them. But for some reason Jae never shows up in those dreams. I'm always riding alone, bending down like this and staying close to the bike . . ."

Her arms moved forward excitedly and she leaned low for me as if she were on a motorcycle. She grinned. "If I knew I was going to die tomorrow, I'd get on a bike now."

I checked my watch. It was getting close to her departure time, so I asked her about Jean. I summarized the contents of the e-mail she'd sent me, and asked, "Did Jae ever tell you about that period of his life?"

Mokran thought about it for a second. "I think so. He told me about an *ajumma*, but her name wasn't Jean or anything close to it. What was it . . . Anyway, I heard that after what happened to Jae, she joined an organization that counsels teen motorcycle gangs. She also knew Donggyu well."

The puzzle was solved. Jean was Y. I recalled her hollow cheeks as she gave Donggyu a warm hug. When I'd complained about the writing not going well, she advised me to "just listen." Was this actually what she had been telling herself?

I said, "I think I know her . . ."

Mokran asked, "Is it someone you know well?"

It wasn't an easy question to answer. "Hmm . . . I can't say I know her so well . . . yet it feels like I've gotten to know her well . . ."

With fiction, just because you begin with the truth doesn't mean you have the truth, and just because it's fiction doesn't mean it's made up. I read only her one letter, and maybe I knew her now even less than before.

"Why's it so complicated?" said Mokran. "If you know her well, you know her, and if you don't, you don't."

That was when Mokran's father showed up. He barely spoke

to me — whether it was because he was always reserved or because he didn't like me, I couldn't tell. She grabbed her unfinished coffee and stood up. As I walked to the parking lot after we parted, I fiddled with the cell phone in my pocket. I debated whether or not to call Y, but finally I decided not to. She had said everything she needed to in her letter, and my novel was my reply.

I got in, started the car, and returned home. As I exited the airport expressway and entered Seoul, I began spotting motorcycles. Delivery service men in black helmets and protective gear sped ahead as soon as the lights changed. They looked like cyborgs. When I was nearly home, a pizza delivery guy suddenly zoomed out from a side street. The guy in a blue uniform met my eyes briefly with cool indifference. As soon as he realized that I'd hit the brake and was slowing down, he leaned forward and sped ahead. The white exhaust of burning engine oil blinded me for a moment, and then it dissipated. The motorcycle had vanished.

Few people still remember that massive motorcycle rally. The motorcycle rallies have continued annually, but they never replicate the madness of that year. Instead they became duller and duller. Lieutenant Pak's report focused on preventive measures rather than cracking down on the rallies. After implementing the changes, the police response became more efficient. They drew up a blacklist with the kids who took part in rallies. An official warning note was sent to them the night before a major rally, pressuring them to stay home, and the police texted warning messages repeatedly to kids who had a record of participating. The game changed further when the courts deemed motorcycles an accessory to crime and began confiscating them. For the teenage bikers, having their motorcycles confiscated equaled losing their entire inheritance. But most biker groups blamed the waning popularity of motorcycle rallies to Jae's absence. The massive rally that Jae had led became legend. The nights before every Independence Movement Day and Liberation Day, rumors would circulate that Jae was still alive, and people prophesied that he would reappear the night of the motorcycle rally.

The worst of winter is passing and the most impatient of trees have already started budding. Late at night, as the northwesterly winds rattle the windows, I sit down at my desk to write "The End" on the manuscript that I had struggled with for so long. Looking back I see how much help I had finishing it, and I want to acknowledge those people and thank them here. But if there is only one person I could thank, it would be Donggyu. Because of him, I was able to discover the infinite, invisible wilderness spinning out from beneath us. I pray he rests in peace.